Also available from Unsung Stories

WHIRLWIND ROMANCE

SAM THOMPSON

UNSUNG
STORIES

Published by Unsung Stories

3 Rosslyn Road
London E17 9EU, United Kingdom

www.unsungstories.co.uk

First edition published in 2022
First impression

Paperback ISBN: 978-1912658206
ePub ISBN: 978-1912658213

Edited by Dan Coxon
Proofreading by Jonathan Oliver
Cover artwork by Guenter Zimmermann
Cover design by Vince Haig
Text design by Cox Design Limited
Typesetting by Vince Haig

Printed in the UK by Clays Ltd, Elcograf S.p.A.

CONTENTS

For Sadhbh, Odhrán, Oisín and Caoileann

WHERE YOU ARE

I don't know. It is only seconds since you were here, maybe half a minute. We are in that gap of moments where this will no doubt turn out fine. Something I'll tell your mother about, the story of a passing fright and not the point on which our lives all turn. I run ten strides along the pavement and twenty back the other way. Teenage gaggle, slow old couple, fundraiser grinning, ponderous backpackers, slender neck and nice brown hair, drunk man, all beside the point. You're not here.

We came into town for some errands – your hair wanted cutting, and I thought we would visit the bookshop to see if I could coax you to a new bedtime story – but my plans went wrong almost at once. You were so distressed by the barber touching your head that I paid and carried you out of the shop with the job half done. I maintained a rigid calm as you struggled and screamed. You're too big to lift nowadays, and I could feel I had wrenched my back.

Out on the pavement I crouched in close, held your hands and asked you to breathe. You twisted away from me, rolling your eyes, pretending I was not there. Was it really too much to expect, I wanted to ask you, an outing to the shops like normal people? By now you were limp, sliding to the pavement with a false, insolent grin on your face.

You were three years old when you stopped making eye contact. When we came into your room in the morning, you would no longer hug us or say hello. You flinched when we touched you, and rubbed our kisses out. For a few months we pushed it, demanding you look at us and answer when spoken to, but it could not be done without giving you pain. Soon enough we adapted. We chose to love you for this above all. We told one another that it made you yourself, this difficulty: that you would go far because you were yourself and would not be swayed. We decided we had seen it in the first moments of your life, when you lay in your mother's arms and gave me a long stare before you cried.

I only took a few steps along the street. I didn't mean to leave you. I was going to have a word with myself and turn around, calm and capable. At the same time what I wanted was to make you feel how I felt.

I shut my eyes, took a breath, and turned to find you gone.

As I began to run, I tripped on a paving slab and nearly went headlong. What a clown. When I was younger I thought growing up would mean finding my balance. And then you came, which meant I must be grown up, but I am more unbalanced than ever, I find. As I ran I was back in the first weeks of your life, when the things I learned from you were very big and simple and strange. When I held you and felt how your flesh was fitted so neat and close on your soul. Even now, sometimes, when you're tired or sad or thoughtful and your face is unguarded, I can glimpse your first self, still there and still true. Each time I make a promise that I am never going to forget it.

I'm back on the spot where I had you last. My lungs are raw, and I think we're past the stage when running around will do much good. Attention is catching here. Claims will be laid. I'm not clear on what comes next. I project a future in which we never see you or hear of you again, in which your life unfolds in circumstances that we never know and you have to become a different person from the person you were going to be.

When you were five years old, your teacher called us in for a meeting. She was tactful. She avoided the formal language, and it took us some time to work out what she was trying to say. Later we would learn that this is one of the classic routes to a diagnosis. Traits unremarked at home become obvious at school. You had trouble dealing with new environments and changes in routine; your motor skills were a concern; you found it hard to read social situations and empathise with other children, and you did not make friends. It was a minor issue in the scheme of things, she said. We knew she was right, and on the way home we agreed to keep it in perspective.

To start announcing that I've lost you seems crassly dramatic. I do not want to give that much ground. As I take out my phone, I glance between these shopfronts, down an alleyway blocked by bins. A kind of alcove is formed by a chained-over side entrance, and a small wretched figure is standing there. It's you.

Your face is covered in tears and snot and you're still crying. When I reach you I go down on one knee and hug you hard, and surely this should be enough to bring us round, to dissolve all our bad feelings and bad behaviour in the sheer fact that we're together again. But that's not how it works. You are stiff in my arms, as if you do not know how to be held, and you are not getting any less upset. Your agitation feeds on itself. Now you are shaking, trying to pull away from me and cling on at the same time, flapping an arm. A family has stopped at the corner to watch us. Young parents with a girl your age and a toddler in a pushchair. The parents are uneasy, not quite sure what's going on. I could not give a fuck what these people think of us, but they matter anyway because they stand for something, some shame in me I cannot root out.

I said that we choose to love you for the difficult things most of all, but that's not true, is it? It's a lie I was telling to make myself feel better. Let me try again. Here is how I love you. Kneeling on the hard ground, scared and angry, fighting to hold on. I am holding myself at seven years old, as if by squeezing tight enough I could mould him into someone new.

I get up and pull you past the watchers, along the street. We must look mad, and I wonder if being mad means not caring whether you look it. I am holding your hand harder than I need to, squeezing the small bones together. I make you go faster than you are able and jerk your arm when you stumble. You are sobbing and panicking. I cannot see how you are ever going to forgive me.

Your mother and I made a promise. You were going to live in a world that would not make sense and where the others would know rules that for you were kept hidden. You were going to fail with people and not know why. Seeing this, we made a promise that here, in the space between the three of us, you would always be understood. We would recognise you for the boy that you are.

I do not keep my promises. As I pull you along I am talking to you and over you, explaining why you are wrong to be upset and why it is unacceptable for you to behave in this way. I seem to think that if I keep insisting you will snap out of it, snap out of being as you are. My tone is one of immense forbearance but the edge of each word is vicious. There are two people in the world I dare speak to like this: you and me.

I stop hauling us through the crowd and find a recess between some bike stands and a railing. I sit down on wet pavement with my back against the wall and hold you on my lap. You are too upset to keep still, you cannot hear me, but I hold you, pinning your arms to your sides as we did when you were a week old and we swaddled you to soothe your cries. You stop fighting. I pull you closer. I feel the heat of your scalp through your hair.

In the first weeks of your life I put my cheek against your face and spoke to you, and the words did not matter. Language was going to happen to you but it had not happened yet, which meant I could say anything at all. I wonder now if those were the truest conversations we are ever going to have.

When I relax my embrace you stay where you are, exhausted, and your weight settles into me. You hitch and sniffle. Soon you are asleep. Your head lolls and for an instant your eyes open and seek me out. Your gaze is big and dark and placid. Eyes close.

I am mumbling words in your ear but I do not know what I am saying. This is how it is. I speak in the hope that one day I will start to listen. I say what I do not yet know.

Your body is heavy and hot. Even in sleep you are breathing in sobs. After a few minutes you wet yourself, and the warmth spreads through your clothes and mine. I work my shoulder around to support your head better. I watch spectators moving past. The urine goes cold. Soon I will need to free my hand, but for now let's stay. We can stay as long as you like. I will hold you, but not too hard. I speak in your ear. I make a promise.

WHIRLWIND ROMANCE

In her lunch break Fern walked over to the park. Groups of students were shouting and staggering about, drunk or pretending to be. It was Freshers' Week. It always seemed to be Freshers' Week, and come November it would be exactly twelve years since she met Jamie. Two girls and two boys ran towards her with their arms linked, so she moved to the edge of the path. She sat down on a bench, got out a tissue and blew her nose. Twelve years had passed and nothing had changed. She was going to get old like this.

Her last appointment of the day was with Rana, a five-year-old with an unusual pattern of speech difficulties. She spent half an hour practising consonant sounds with the boy while his mother watched from the other side of the room, pained by his struggle. He was a sweet child and he enjoyed the word games, though he grew fractious from exhaustion in the last ten minutes of the session. Afterwards Fern finished her paperwork, then knocked on Angela's office door and handed in her notice. She had decided to accept a job down south, she explained. No, she said, purely for personal reasons. Yes, it was very sudden and hard to understand.

With the decision made her flat had a different look to it. She saw how quickly she would be able to pack up the clothes and the books, and how little changed the place would be when she had gone. A net of fairy lights tacked above the bed, some scented candles on the mantelpiece: was this all? And yet she had no desire to move to a new city, because if she belonged anywhere it was here. Almost everyone she had studied with had moved away after graduating, but she had stayed. She liked the town, with its steep streets, nice old buildings, brisk weather and walkable size, and she liked knowing her way around.

And there was Jamie, who had been here all along. In truth she had stayed so that she could keep on being hurt. Hurt by hope, hurt by disappointment, hurt above all by her failure to make sense of her own behaviour. She was tired of it now. The sensible course of action, she knew, was not to make herself vulnerable for a second longer, simply to pick up and vanish without trying to say goodbye.

Jamie did not use a phone, but it was usually possible to track him down by visiting the places where he worked. She called in at the Cancer Research shop where he did a few shifts each week, but he was not there. He had an irregular gig as an assistant technician at the little black box theatre in the university, where the undergraduate drama sorts made fun of him behind his back. Today, several of them were lounging as usual on the sofas in the foyer, drinking take-out coffees and giving one another back rubs. No, they said, gazing at her with compassion, he hadn't been in. Sorry, poppet, wish we could help.

That left one place to try. Fern walked along the embankment and crossed the river, then skirted a supermarket car park. At the end of a row of Victorian workers' houses, an L-shaped lane led to a yard where an old Volvo estate rested on bricks. Nettles filled the wheel arches and poked through the radiator grille. It was evening now. The sky was pale but the light would soon be gone. Fern crossed the yard and tried the door.

The room inside was large, but it was crowded with junk to the point of claustrophobia. Old furniture filled most of the space. A light bulb glowed under a shaggy lampshade, picking out a nest of obsolete computer cables and a shoebox filled with tarnished cutlery. Fern had never been able to tell whether this place was an actual rag-and-bone shop or simply a hoarder's den, but it made no difference. Perhaps Jamie was Lionel Gull's employee or perhaps he gave his time for nothing. Perhaps he was an assistant or a carer or something in between. Whatever the nature of the situation, the old man had a hold over him.

As she was wondering whether to call out, Jamie came down the stairs. He had a couple of days' worth of beard and his hair needed cutting. He was wearing his grungy jeans and a flannel shirt she had not seen before. When he noticed her, his face turned sober. She had learned long ago that it was impossible to prepare for these encounters. She might abstain for a fortnight, a month, six months, but sooner or later they always came face to face again. She could tell herself in advance that she would regret it, but what surprised her every time was how pleased she was to see him. Perhaps that in itself accounted for the course her life had taken.

He came over in the way he always did, hastening forward and then checking himself just out of reach. The crinkles formed at the corners of his eyes. This would not take long, Fern reminded herself.

'Do you have a minute?'

Before Jamie could answer, a noise came from the alcove under the stairs. It might have been a cough or a grunt of derision. Gull was slumped in the ruin of an armchair. He had been sitting there, watching, since Fern came in. His moustaches parted to show his awful teeth. He reached up and raised his toque, then set it back on his head.

'In private,' Fern said.

Two worlds: the yellow headlamps of the traffic passing over the bridge, the underside of the bridge floodlit blue. Fern and Jamie walked on the embankment. The cruelty was that it still felt right. Their feet found a rhythm and she curbed the impulse to take his hand. On their first night, when she had known him for three or four hours, she had got Jamie to play a game she had seen in a film, hopping ten paces along the pavement and telling her a fact about himself for each hop. That had been the idea, at least, though Jamie had struggled to come up with much beyond the information that he had lived in one of the halls of residence last year and that he was an only child. Thinking of it now made her squirm. Even at the time she had known she was laying herself open, but she had not minded. She had been so sure they were at the beginning of something. She had been right. They had had fifteen days together, and it turned out that you could easily pay with twelve years of your life for fifteen days spent falling in love.

'So that's it,' Fern said.

It was tempting to keep talking, to wade into explanations and excuses. On the other hand, she could get angry now if she tried. She could ask what was wrong with him, tell him how badly she wanted to shake him, demand to know why he had wasted her time. There was no point. He always escaped blame. When you felt he had broken a promise, you found he had never quite made it in the first place. After their fifteen days he had disappeared. At first she had thought he was only avoiding her, but no one had seen him and soon it was apparent that he had dropped out of his degree. Eight months later she saw him in one of the little streets behind the covered market. He was sitting on a step at the back entrance of a shop. She flattered herself that most people would not have recognised him under the shaggy hair. He was dressed out of a charity shop and looked much older. But he smiled at her, and they went for a cup of tea and a sandwich. Only a hint of distance in his manner told her it was not all right to ask where he had been.

Now Jamie was interested in her plans, wanting to know about the new job, where she was going to live, when she'd be moving, whether she knew anyone down there. He was a friend being supportive of a new venture, encouraging her as she planned the next stage. She could go along with that, she supposed. She had learned to respond to the cues. After finding him again, she had never pressed him to discuss what had happened between them. She could not find a way into the subject, so instead she pieced together the way things were going to be from now on. How they would run into one another every week or two around the city centre; how they would do their best to behave like old friends and no more; how he would tell her readily about the bits and pieces of work he found, but would be cagey about where he was living; how she would keep glimpsing Lionel Gull in the background, but would never be able to work out the nature of his involvement; how, over twelve years, five boyfriends would come to nothing, because with each of them she would learn again that she was not free to fall in love.

They turned onto her street and walked down to the entrance to her building. The lamp across the road was malfunctioning, stuttering on and off so that the empty street staggered between two forms of itself.

'This is me,' she said, as if he didn't know.

She searched for her keys, then stopped and looked at him. He moved towards her. The lamp flickered, then held steady, as their hands entangled.

> • <

Jamie kept to the middle of the road, tracked by shadows that shrank under him then lurched ahead. The sky told him dawn was near. He had left his shoes in her flat and his feet were numb and bloody.

His enemies were gleeful, several of the boldest flinging themselves at the boundary as if they hoped to break through. Their voices were all around. The lesser ministers chattered among themselves, giggling over his mistake, while their superiors crowded in to pester him. Was it worth it? asked the Gadfly, and Doghead answered with coarse sarcasm that of course it was worth it for a few hours spooning on top of her bedclothes, mouthing lies then falling asleep. Sister Dust and Sister Dew sighed, clattered their steel claws and began to describe the atrocities they would inflict on Fern as soon as they got the chance.

He slipped and fell, skinning his palms on the tarmac. Bottle Sal chuckled in his ear and asked what she thought of him now. The Gentleman Thief observed that if Jamie were to strike his head firmly and repeatedly on the surface of the road, it would amount to the solution to all his difficulties and all hers as well. Jamie hesitated, and the gallery fell silent. They hooted in disapproval as he got up, brushing away the gravel embedded in his hands.

Enemies pressed in, scraping at the walls of their world. Over time he had taught most of them to be wary, but now that was undone. The Gadfly coughed, died, rotted and was reborn as a nest of maggots which asked in a hundred tiny mocking voices whether it had been worth it. Doghead began to masturbate ostentatiously while Blithe Spirit cavorted along its endless hall of mirrors. The Lepidopterist droned the litany of Jamie's failures and humiliations.

All this enthusiasm manifested as a pain in his head, so intense that he cried out. He sat on the kerb and tried to breathe. There was no telling how seriously he had compromised the balance of things. It was inexcusable. He had known that Fern's place in the scheme was vital. His enemies had always understood that their greatest opportunity lay with her. Twelve years ago he had met Fern and the things had arrived, nameless then, crooning and sniggering as they swarmed around her, scrabbling at the catches of what was real.

Sodium lamplight vibrated. He ran madly along the streets until he came to the park. The gate was locked for the night, so he climbed the railings and slithered through mud to the sunken garden. Here, in clammy twilight, it was easier to recover some control. Far too late for that, old boy, said the Gentleman Thief, but Jamie went back to the first disciplines Gull had taught him. How to breathe, how to be here. When the old man had found him, he had been exhausted and about to give up. He had been running and hiding for weeks. Gull had shown him the rudiments of self-preservation and, later, guided him through the researches by which he had learned to keep his tormentors at bay.

Now they clamoured at him but did nothing else. For all their crowing it seemed that his mistake had not been fatal. The Gentleman Thief clicked his tongue and strolled away. One of the maggots finished devouring its ninety-nine siblings and metamorphosed into the Gadfly's mature form, which pulled a face before drifting into the murk. Doghead belched and wandered off. The others followed suit.

Don't make no difference, mate, said Bottle Sal as she went. Boss wants to know. The Sisters sighed in mock-sympathy. He's got your scent, they said. He's on your trail.

'Who?'

They laughed and were gone. He stood alone in the centre of the park. The sky was cobwebbed, the moon a luminous thumbprint. The pain in his head began to ease, and he became aware of a shift in the substance of things. A swell like the disturbance of water when something very large and very deep stirs and begins to rise.

Day was breaking when he reached Gull's place. He had a stitch and his feet were bleeding freely. When he tried to explain what had happened, his throat was so raw that the words would not come. Gull seemed to understand anyway. He hauled himself from the armchair where he had evidently spent the night, limped through to the kitchen, and filled the kettle.

What was coming was a different order of enemy. It had no name that Jamie or Gull had been able to find out. They had tried various alternatives – the Thin One, Poker Face, Glory Bill, the Maimed – but none had proved accurate, and they had been forced to accept that it might be truly nameless. What little they knew about it was guesswork from the clues Jamie had gathered. A dozen crows blowing over salt flats like cinders off a bonfire; white smoke falling upward in solid shapes like the bodies of gymnasts; a sculpted frieze in sunset colours, processing behind black trees and dissolving to night. Fragments like these, scattered through his childhood and adolescence, had been traces of the enemy, but they had only come together on the morning after his first night with Fern. He had kissed her goodbye at the corner of her street and walked away towards the city centre, an involuntary happiness branching through his body to blossom from his head. Even then he had wondered if it was too much – if it was a reckless invitation – and although the days that followed were the best he had known, he felt that something dangerous was close. The Friday night crowds were roiling currents that twisted and thickened, then thinned away. As they walked under a bridge, a car full of young males crawled past, and the front passenger called out *Did you pay for her, you cunt?* The young man had a well-proportioned face and a look of happy confidence in himself.

Gull made two mugs of tea. Indifferent to Jamie's agitation, he added milk and sugar and squeezed out the bags with a spoon. He blew across his mug and drained it in one long swallow. He wiped his beard with the back of his hand.

'Best get on,' he said.

In the front shop, the old man shuffled around indecisively, stopping every so often to root among the junk or to make some small adjustment, shifting the angle of a picture frame propped in a corner, opening a drawer and closing it again. Jamie hung back, recognising this behaviour as

Gull's way of preparing for an act of magic. Early in their association Gull had used more elaborate rituals, chalking sigils on the floor and muttering phrases that belonged to no ordinary language, but over time he had allowed Jamie to understand that such niceties were not essential. When he tried something difficult, Gull preferred to do without props.

The old man stooped, groaning with the effort, and rifled under a dresser. When he straightened he was holding a kitchen knife. He tested the edge with his thumb and rubbed at the rust on the blade. Then, satisfied, he offered the handle to Jamie.

'You'll want to be quick.'

Gull waved away Jamie's objections. No time. It was true: the enemy's closeness made his ears pop. Gull was asking far too much, but there was no time to reason with him or beg him to find another way. In Jamie's hands the knife was an object from another planet. The room was dim and quiet but in the other world huge waveforms were slopping through.

Gull limped over to his armchair and made himself comfortable. He took out a handkerchief and spread it over his face as if he were getting ready for a nap. The familiar enemies had crept out of their hiding places, afraid to come closer but eager to see Jamie dragged into the abyss. The surging waveforms became a vortex which gave birth to the nameless presence, and at that moment Gull carried out the act of magic he had prepared.

The room was empty. The enemies gibbered, confused by the absence of their master. Gull sat motionless in the armchair with the handkerchief spread on his face. Jamie adjusted his grip on the knife. One of Gull's great subjects was the difference between the real and the unreal. It is true that one thing exists and the other doesn't, the old man liked to say, but don't let it fool you.

Jamie padded over to the armchair and lifted the handkerchief. The old man's face was tranquil. To all appearances Lionel Gull had fallen asleep. Jamie touched the figure's shoulder, half-hoping they had been wrong about everything, but when the eyes opened what looked at him was ancient and hungry and furious at the trap it had fallen into. Its hand seized Jamie's wrist and twisted with horrible strength until he dropped the knife.

> • <

Fern crossed the river and skirted the car park. It was madness to chase after him again, but that hardly mattered now. She felt a detached interest in discovering how much of a fool she actually was, how much pointless heartache she was willing to take.

For a few hours last night she had believed things had changed. As they lay on her bed, both too surprised to do more than hold one another, she had laughed at how simple it had turned out to be. A cheap trick by the universe: if you leave then you can stay. Jamie had grown serious and started to tell her how sorry he was for everything, but she had hushed him. What they had to think about now was the future.

She had woken a couple of hours later to find him pulling his arm free. When she sat up, something like panic crossed his face. He wished her good luck with the move and the new job. He fell over himself to get out of the flat, leaving her to drift back to the bedroom and stare numbly at the shoes he had left lying at the foot of the bed.

She walked down the L-shaped lane and crossed the yard. A crash came from Gull's place. Fern went in.

The rag-and-bone shop had been destroyed. The floor was strewn with pieces of mirror and crockery. Half the furniture had been knocked over or smashed, as if a large, frantic animal had been searching for a way out. Jamie stood at the end of the room, looking as if he had been in a road accident. His face was bloody. He was stooping and he kept a hand pressed to his left side.

The dead body of Lionel Gull lay on the floor with its legs tangled in the cord of a standard lamp. The lamp had fallen but its bulb was still glowing. Gull seemed to have died by suffocating inside the large, clear plastic bag that was wrapped around his head. Jamie took a step forward and fell against a dresser, dislodging a long shard of glass. Fern went to him and helped him get his balance. He flinched at her touch, then put an arm around her and let her take his weight.

They looked down at Gull's body. The polythene death mask was drawn tight on the features, preserving an expression of inhuman malevolence. The fallen lamp faltered and went out. For two minutes they stood in silence.

They chose the same moment to speak.

'What did you see?' he said.

And she said: 'Where shall we start?'

THE RED SONG

I remember spring rain dripping from the balconies, and streets blocked with the rubbish that went uncollected for months. I remember heavy skies, bright evenings, wet light. I remember the Yellow Rose in all its forms: flags, placards, posters and graffiti, adorning the city from the shutters of the Old Town to the concrete slabs in front of the ruined palace.

I remember Hesperus.

The fellowship carried no formal teaching responsibilities, but over my stay I was meant to offer three talks on topics relating to my research. The turnout was surprising for my first seminar, with a good thirty people filling the classroom to hear me talk about Fallon Herm and the Nine Songs. I told them the university's manuscript collection was a treasure trove and that I hoped my translations would play a small part in bringing Herm's vision to the wider world. I showed them a length of string in which, to the best of my ability, I had made a phrase in Astic knot-script. I was respectful to the point of flattery: I was lecturing them about their national poet.

One student waited afterwards. A short, serious young man with broad shoulders, dark eyes and a shabby overcoat. I had seen him smoking roll-ups around the Arts Faculty. In fast, inaccurate English, he told me that Fallon Herm had been a great man and what I had said was true, nothing was more important than Herm's work because it held the future of the Hesp nation. I was not sure I had quite said this, but he was nodding fiercely, enthusiasm spilling from him like heat. Then he let his fringe fall into his eyes. He must apologise, he said. He was a fool to waste the time of such a scholar as myself. Unsure whether he was teasing me, I gave him a brisk smile and gathered up my papers. All at once he looked so disconsolate that I asked his name.

'Petar Bron,' he said, brightening. 'An honour, Dr Hardy.'

'Flora.'

We bought coffees from the catering stand in the basement hall of the faculty, and spent the next hour talking about Fallon Herm. I did my best to answer his questions, though he knew at least as much about Herm's work as I did, and obviously cared about it with a passion I could not pretend to match. The first thing Bron had done after the revolution was enrol here for courses in Astic literature, he told me. It had not been possible for him to attend the university before, but now he had taken his chance. Hadn't he been tempted to study something more useful, I asked, like information technology or engineering or business? He gave me a sharp look, then grinned and wagged his finger as if to show that he was wise to my mischief.

We walked through the campus, a sprawling, monotonous environment of tower blocks, catwalks, tunnels and stairwells finished in raw concrete. When Barris Kess had seized power in Hesperus, he had closed down the Schools of the Hidden, the learned societies that had existed since before records began. Fifteen years later he had decided, with his typical immunity to irony, that Hesperus ought to have a great university: he had a district of the city bulldozed and replaced with a vast campus designed by an architect of the Brutalist school.

We paused by a slab-like building decorated with a mural of the Yellow Rose.

'And you,' Bron said. 'How did you come here?'

I explained as best I could that I had taken a module called Introduction to Astic Language and Literature in my final undergraduate year. At that time I spoke no Astic and knew nothing about Hesp culture, but the obscurity of the subject appealed to me. I got a high mark and decided to apply for graduate study.

'I understand,' he said. 'You learn our poets, you learn Fallon Herm, and you know you must come here one day.'

I agreed this was more or less the story, though in truth I'd always had mixed feelings about Herm's writing. The poetry was dense, ponderous and obsessed with Hesper's past, cluttered with mystical ideas that had been out of date long before Kess came to power. But Herm suited me as a research topic. I could spend whole days in a productive trance of translation, and there was plenty of work to be done tracking down his allusions and mapping out the historical, political and cultural contexts of his writing. After four years and nine months, I submitted a doctoral thesis entitled *Violence, Renewal and the Hesp Esoteric Tradition in the Narrative Verse of Fallon Herm*, and I was in the process of developing it into a monograph when the revolution came.

'The revolution,' Bron said. 'You see the Hesp people rise up.'

I nodded. The Hesp uprising had been abrupt, unforeseen and freakishly successful. One day in April, the first crowds gathered in the Victorious People's Square in the centre of Hesperus. Ten weeks later the civil war was over and Barris Kess was dead, hanged beside his sons and lieutenants in that same square, to which the revolutionaries had restored its old name, the Place of Shadows. For a few months Hesper was at the top of every international news bulletin and the Hesp people were heroes. They had liberated themselves and the world was on their side.

When the revolution began to appear on the news, my first response was a sort of jealousy – I had always thought of Hesper as mine alone – but rationally I knew there was no way current events could undermine the validity of my research. On the contrary, I could not have hoped for a better moment to be writing an academic monograph on the work of a difficult Astic poet who had died twenty years ago in one of Kess's prisons: it looked almost fashionable.

'So you come,' Bron said. 'And now you will join in the future of Hesper.'

Walking into a courtyard, we came face to face with the Yellow Rose again. The Rose had been the Hesp flag in the times before Kess, and in the revolution it had been reborn as a rallying symbol for the rebels. This mural was an elaborate piece of work: the huge, stylised flower in the centre of the wall was surrounded by portraits of men and women who must have perished during the war, and a rainbow arched above the Rose, bearing Astic script that read *Freedom*.

'I hope so,' I said.

Bron was staring at me, grave as a boy.

'I know it.'

> • <

'Who is this person? What do you know about him? And, hang on, because—'

The image stuttered and smeared. Video calling never worked properly here, but I knew what Seb was trying to say. We had split up a few weeks before I came to Hesperus, but we spoke now and then. He never got tired of reminding me of the dangers to Westerners in the city.

Seb and I had met at university and led a settled domestic life for several years, him working for a consultancy firm while I did my PhD. Once I submitted the thesis and started taking teaching assistant stints wherever I could, there were periods when we did not see one another, but he said that if I wanted to pursue my career then he supported me. It was only after I interviewed for the fellowship that he began to get rattled. The offer came with a sheaf of risk assessment forms and security briefing documents. Seb read them aloud, his voice rising in alarm. There was high likelihood of political demonstrations, rallies, violent clashes and terrorism. There had been celebratory gunfire since the revolution and a number of fatalities had occurred as a result of rounds falling from the sky. Daily life in the capital was broadly back to normal but the security situation was unpredictable. Large numbers of weapons were in circulation. Foreign visitors were advised to keep a low profile, avoid crowds, move away from disturbances in the street, treat militia with respect, be patient if stopped at roadblocks, avoid travelling in private vehicles and not go out after nine o'clock in the evening.

Seb could not believe I would be so irresponsible. After a few days of sulking, he told me that we could get married if I'd forget about Hesperus. The following night I moved out of his flat.

Now the image on my screen caught up with itself, and a snatch of his voice came through.

'—only saying I care what you—'

The call dropped. I shut the laptop and walked over to the Arts Faculty to meet Bron. He was going to show me around the Old Town. He had been appalled to discover that I was working on my translation without having visited the ceremonial sites for myself.

Bron was at ease in the streets. He paused and moved in a dance with the pedal bikes, scooters and taxis that cut across our path. In the Lane of the Veils he bantered with the DVD sellers, and we paused to watch some children street-dancing on flattened cardboard boxes. Weaving through the crowds was a social process: every few steps he exchanged a hand clasp, a comment or a joke with a passer-by. Apparently when two Hesp passed on the street they considered themselves already mid-conversation.

The Old Town was a square mile of alleys and wynds embedded in the centre of modern Hesperus. Here and there, pieces of carved stone were set into the walls – pillars, archways, medallions and caryatids, ornate and weathered – as if the ancient streets had been built from the ruins of yet more ancient structures. Tiny cafés and tobacco shops served their customers through windows. Yellow Rose bunting was strung between the iron balconies overhead.

We crossed the Calendar Place, where a bomb had gone off a fortnight ago, killing six, injuring seventeen and destroying one of the city's oldest landmarks. A group calling itself the Hesp Nationalist Vanguard had claimed responsibility. The Calendar Spire had been a spindly stone campanile in the centre of the square. Now teenage boys played on the rubble, showing one another their mobile phones. The paving slabs underfoot were huge and worn, each carved with a unique figure of notches and curved lines.

Walking through an alleyway we met a group of people in masks. Twenty or thirty of them surrounded us quickly and moved on. The masks were all the same: wedge shapes cut from varnished leather, featureless except for small round eyeholes.

'Who are they?'

Bron looked nonplussed.

'People of Hesperus,' he said. 'My brothers and sisters.'

We skirted the Place of Shadows, where hundreds of gulls squabbled. A tunnel-like street sloped downwards, breaking into flights of steps in several places, and brought us to an amphitheatre.

'Here,' Bron said, proud of himself.

We were in the Place of the Songs. The little amphitheatre was supposed to be the exact centre of the Old Town, and it had a strong claim to be the oldest surviving site in Hesperus. Some theories claimed that when the site of the city had been nothing but a plain of black clay and a nameless river crawling down to the sea, the Song-Place had already been in use.

A bearded man was sitting in the stands with old newspapers and plastic carrier bags spread around him. When he saw us he got up and began to shout in jumbled

Astic. He worked his way down the stands and crossed the arena, pointing and gesticulating. His clothes were rags.

'He's crazy,' Bron said.

As we walked out of the Place, I wanted to reassure him that I understood. The man was obviously unwell. But Bron only shook his head, his mood spoiled.

'Crazy man.'

> • <

A week later I gave my second seminar. It was a success: the numbers held up and the audience listened appreciatively to my interpretation of the evidence relating to the Prelude Chorus of the Red Song. In later eras the climax of the Red Song festival had become purely symbolic, but most scholars agreed that in its earliest form the Song had concluded, in literal fashion, with a ritualised killing. I argued that the Prelude Chorus was a vital element of this cultural work, not only because it marked the beginning of the festival period, but because it was the occasion on which two Hesp citizens were selected to perform the main roles, three days later, in the Red Song proper. The citizens would volunteer, but the parts would be assigned by lot: a black marble would identify the protagonist whose demise was to mark the climax, while a white marble identified the antagonist whose role was to carry out the sacrifice, using the final line of the Song – *As Above, So Below* – for the act of ceremonial strangulation. Once the roles were assigned, I explained, the actors removed their masks to show their separation from the citizen chorus, and were led away from the scene of the Prelude to be kept in purifying isolation until the night of the Song itself. One or two details of my account might, perhaps, have been accused of straying into speculation, but I gave myself the latitude, knowing that my audience would appreciate some touches of colour.

Bron did not attend the seminar, but I found him in the library that afternoon. He was sitting at one of the ground-floor carrels, frowning into a battered paperback. I walked across and touched his shoulder.

'I want to show you something,' I said.

Like the rest of the campus, the library was much larger than it needed to be, and the upper floors were virtually unused. One middle-aged man worked at a desk among the broken furniture and empty shelves on the fourth floor. He was plump and balding, with thick bifocals and a drooping moustache. He was always here. As we passed him, Bron grew tense.

'Do you know him?'

Bron nodded.

The top floor was a warren of shelves and storerooms, lit by bulbs on timer switches. One cupboard contained hundreds of copies of *The Beloved Teachings of Supreme General Barris Kess, Brother of the People, Father of the Unending Revolution and Leader of the Scientific Socialist Republic of Hesper.* I had thought of taking one as a souvenir – until recently, a detailed knowledge of the book's contents had been compulsory for every citizen of Hesper – but I had left them alone. I did not know what would happen nowadays if I was found with a copy in my possession.

I led Bron to the Special Collections room, where the Herm archive was kept. A key to this room and a desk under its murky window were two of the benefits of the fellowship.

When Bron saw the cardboard crates marked with the poet's name, he exclaimed under his breath.

The material spanned Herm's career. Bundles of the underground pamphlets in which his earliest dissident lyrics had appeared, typescripts at all stages of completion, manuscript notes in cheap exercise books, scribbles and doodles on used envelopes and scraps of cardboard. Much of the paper was speckled with damp. I had found drafts of *Notes for a Requiem*, *Notes for a Delusion* and *Notes for a Betrayal*, and of *Night Walks* and *Dawn Dreams*. There was masses of research for Herm's seriocomic variations on Hesp folk tales, and for the middle-period works in which he had delved more deeply into the myth cycles. I had come across what looked like sketch-work for *Death of a Fruit Merchant* and *Astrid in the Underworld*.

I let Bron look through a couple of crates. He was tentative, lifting pages as if they might crumble to dust. While he was busy, I began to unpack the prize exhibit.

Herm had been preoccupied with the Nine Songs throughout his writing life, and the project of recreating the ancient cycle for modern Hesper had been with him for decades. Most of his versions of the Songs had circulated in samizdat during the last twenty years of his life, and after his death they had been published by presses outside Hesper. But his adaptation was incomplete: his versions of 'The Birth of Phellida' and 'Vernid's Return' were riddled with gaps, and his 'House with Seven Corridors' was a fragment of only two dozen lines. He had never published any part of the final movement in the cycle, the nameless drama that was usually known as the Red Song.

I opened a crate, lifted out a mass of fine cord and unfolded it on the tabletop, with the index-line in the centre and the song-lines extending on both sides like ribs from a spine. Each line was tied with hundreds of knots down its length. Each knot was an example of skilled craft, elaborate and decorative in spite of being so tiny.

'Obviously, it's modern,' I said.

Knot-script was the primordial form of recorded Astic, the system from which, much later, the written script had evolved. I'd had to dig out primers before I could even attempt a transcription. It was baffling that Herm would have tried to compose his work in knot-script – I could hardly imagine a more laborious and pointless undertaking – but there it was. We were looking at the text of the final movement in Fallon Herm's adaptation of the Nine Songs.

'The Red Song,' Bron said.

He gazed at the knotwork and made no attempt to touch it.

'Herm was a songmaker, like the old songmakers,' he said. 'He knew this song would make Hesper new.'

> • <

Barris Kess had destroyed the culture of Hesper because it was a threat to his authority. Art, music and theatre had been cut off at the roots, with artists and scholars killed, imprisoned or forced into exile and silence. Religion had been outlawed under the regime, which was officially atheistic but made Kess himself into a god whose daily worship was compulsory.

So Bron told me, as we walked towards the stone archway that formed one of the entrances to the Old Town. We had ridden the bus across the inner west side of Hesperus: salty drizzle, lethal traffic, shelled-out residential buildings, walls decorated with insulting caricatures of Kess and variations on the Yellow Rose. Bron was talkative today. He was going to introduce me to a man called Esslin Crae, a lifelong friend of Fallon Herm. The two men had been fellow poets when they were young, and before Herm's blacklisting Crae had been instrumental in publishing his early work. For the past forty years Crae had run a bookshop in the Old Town.

'Tyranny is the same wherever it happens,' Bron said, 'and it can happen anywhere in the world. We in Hesper, we have to be ashamed. We have to ask ourselves questions. What was it about us that let it happen here? It's hard for you to understand when you've been free for a thousand years. But it happened in your country too, long ago, and it can happen again, here or there or anywhere, if the people fail to keep it out. It's always the same. The tyrant knows that art, religion, culture and tradition are defences against him, so he kills them. He makes sure that no one has time for these things. Every day under Kess, you're surviving, and that's all. You're competing with your neighbour, wondering how you can stay safe and get food. You don't have time to think about anything else, and besides, you're too afraid. Unless you are a great person like Fallon Herm, who wrote his poems in spite of the cost.'

Bron was quiet for a while, walking in the wet streets. Then he began to talk about the plump researcher we had seen on the fourth floor of the library.

The man's name was Olifer Tepp, and he had once been an essayist and novelist. His name had been well known and much praised in Hesper during the time of Kess. But there was only one way for a writer to prosper under Kess, and that was by betraying every decent principle. Tepp's work had been lies and propaganda. For this he had been richly rewarded, while men of integrity like Fallon Herm, men who spoke the truth, had suffered and died.

'They say that after the revolution we must all start fresh,' Bron said. 'We must forget what went before.'

He wiped his face.

'Good news for Tepp, no?'

The bookshop was in a dark side-street. Bron pushed through the door, jangling a bell, and led me into a room hardly wider than a corridor. Books were stacked against the walls from floor to ceiling. The shopkeeper, an obese, elderly man in a stained aertex shirt, struggled to his feet and clasped Bron's hands.

'Esslin Crae,' Bron said.

I went to shake hands too, but Crae was already beckoning us to the rear of his shop. The back room was a chaos of books, papers and bric-a-brac. It looked as though the old man ate and slept here. He swept a stack of newspapers off a sofa, lifted a pile of dirty plates, and flapped a hand for us to sit down. He fussed with a coffeepot on a stove in the corner.

'So,' Crae said. 'You want to speak with me about Fallon Herm.'

He handed cups to Bron and lowered himself into a revolving chair.

'Why are you here? Why here in my shop, why here in Hesperus?'

Bron began to say something, but Crae ignored him.

'My friend Petar, here, tells me you want to speak with me about Herm because you are *expert* in his work. You are here for *research*.'

Crae slurped from his cup.

'You want me to give you nice stories, I think. You are *expert*, you know already what Herm means in his poems. Yes? I know this from my friend Petar, here.'

Bron fidgeted on the low sofa and tried again to interrupt.

'You want perhaps to hear about the dangers he braved so that he could write?' Crae said. 'What he lost? Or perhaps you want me to tell you it was a happy story in the end, that it was worth it for him?'

He nodded, his eyes disappearing into creases.

'I will not, because you will not understand. Yes, I know how this is. You come to Hesper and they keep you safe in their university, they pay for you, they make sure you see nothing. Then they send you home to say that all is well here in Hesperus. Hurray for the revolution, hurray democracy, hurray for the brave little people of Hesp.'

He had been rolling a cigarette as he spoke, and now he struck a match. I began to explain that he had misunderstood, but he waved my words away with his smoke.

'You are a tourist. You don't know what Herm means in his poems. You waste your time. How long have you been in Hesp? A month? Two months? If you wish to know Herm's meaning you must go out into the streets of Hesperus, you must go to the fields and mountains, you must go to Nycta and Oa. You must live here not for six months but for twenty years, thirty years. Then I will talk to you, yes?'

He laughed, good-humoured, and slapped his knees.

'Come to me and we'll talk!'

He rummaged in a box and brought out a thin paperback, cheaply printed, with Astic text on a dull pink cover. It was a copy of Herm's *An Empty Street*.

'The first collection we made together. First edition. It's for you.'

Shuffling and coughing, Crae saw us to the door of the shop. He slapped Bron's shoulder and bowed to me.

'I wish you well,' he said. 'I hope you enjoy your holiday.'

Bron said little as we walked out of the Old Town and caught the bus back to the university, and I made no attempt to encourage him. Mostly I was angry about the wasted time, and his stupidity. He had expected gratitude for forcing me to meet that unpleasant old man. I could not think why I had agreed to go. Bron was not a person I wanted to spend any time with: he never really understood what I said, and his own talk was dull and repetitive, with a kind of hectoring sincerity that I didn't like at all. It was clear we had nothing to say to one another.

When we reached the entrance to my accommodation block, I nodded a curt goodbye and he scowled back. Then I took his face in my hands and pushed him against the wall.

> • <

We spent the next three days in my living quarters. On the evening of the first day, Bron went out for supplies and came back with spiced-chicken *khrus,* a carton of mint *feni*, a pint of ice cream and five bottles of red wine. As he opened the first bottle, I told him about the vital role that alcohol played in courtship customs in my country. He told me how Kess had once decided that alcoholic drink was inimical to the principles of the People's Scientific Socialist Republic, and had outlawed it overnight. The prohibition had only been enforced for three months, after which Kess lost interest, but in that time a moonshine industry had sprung up in Hesperus. The bootleggers were incompetent, and the hospitals were swamped with people blinded, liver-damaged and otherwise maimed by ethanol poisoning.

On the second day we were still in bed at mid-afternoon. Bron sat up against the headboard, telling me how every revolution in history had been won by heroes and stolen by bastards. He talked about corruption in the provisional government, the improbability of an election being held any time soon, and the need for a return to the origins of Hesp culture and tradition. Nothing would be right in Hesper, Bron said, until the people lived by the Nine Songs again. That was what Fallon Herm had foreseen; that was why he had devoted his genius to giving new life to those ancient ceremonies.

The calendar of archaic Hesperus was organised around the festivals of the Nine Songs. The scholarly consensus was that the Songs had enacted a mythic cycle corresponding with phases in the life of the individual, the city-state and the universe, from childhood through maturity and fruitfulness to leave-taking and last things. The final, unnamed song, the Red Song, was the song of destruction, enacting the purging catastrophe that made the world new so the cycle could begin over again.

'This is Hesper's need,' Bron said. 'We must be newly born.'

I could not help feeling he was taking a romantic view of sacrificial murder. I almost said as much, but I was fogged by last night's wine. I yawned, then slipped under the sheet to see how quickly I could make him stop talking.

I made him smoke his cigarettes out of the window, and on the morning of the third day we leaned on the sill, nursing hangovers and watching the walkway below. At one point

Olifer Tepp waddled directly beneath us. Bron flicked ash towards the pale dome of his head. Watching him disappear towards the library, I felt a kind of pity.

'How does it work?' I asked Bron. 'If he was mixed up with the Kess regime, how can he be walking around as if he's done nothing wrong?'

Bron shook his head.

'Everyone did something under Kess. Everyone has their own story of what they did and why they could not do otherwise. Tepp would tell you he had no choice when he wrote what Kess wanted. When he spread lies, when he justified torture and murder.'

The worst outrage of Tepp's career, Bron said, had been *Vada Cass*, a short book of supposed reportage named for the maximum security prison at Hesperus's southern city limits. The book claimed to be an investigation into rumours about a massacre in the prison. Vada Cass was already a byword for abuse and brutality, but at that time, nine years before Kess's fall, stories were circulating that over a thousand prisoners had been murdered in a day by the prison guards. Street protests had begun to grow, led by the families of the disappeared prisoners. Tepp's narrative concluded that on the day in question, a gang of hardened convicts associated with violent militant groups had captured several guards, stolen weapons from the prison cache, and attempted to incite a riot. Any casualties had been an unavoidable consequence of the brave efforts of security personnel to restore order, Tepp claimed, and more guards than prisoners had been killed. The book was hailed by the regime, and its claims were reproduced in the official sources of news. At the same time the protests were violently suppressed.

'But if that's true…' I paused, not sure what I was trying to say. 'I don't know, shouldn't he be held responsible?'

Bron scowled.

'Who would do it? What could be the punishment?'

On the fourth day, Bron told me he was due at work. He was a kitchen porter at the Commodore, the ugly hotel on the Avenue of the Drowned. Once he had gone, I dozed, showered, dressed and left my room to put in an afternoon at the library. It was only when I got to the Special Collections room that I discovered I did not have my key.

> • <

I was back in my room, searching under the bed, when my laptop chimed.

It was Seb. I hesitated before accepting the call. I was not in the mood to be instructed on my personal safety, but he did not seem to be phoning for an argument: he waved awkwardly at the camera, lost for words.

'It's good to see you,' he said. 'You look good.'

Instead of a shirt and tie he was in an old hoodie, which with his rumpled hair reminded me of the Seb I had known as a student. I asked how he was doing.

'Oh, I'm fine.'

Work was fine, he said, London was fine. Not much was going on. He'd been missing me lately. His eyes shifted around below camera level.

'When you get home, I was thinking we should, you know. Get together.'

'Okay,' I said, unsure what he was getting at. 'If you like.'

He smiled, looking relieved.

'Great,' he said. 'That's great.'

He was looking forward to having me back, he added. It was a long time to wait, but it would be worth it.

I looked around the room in the hope that my Special Collections key had been lying in full view all along. In the blocky image his face grew bigger.

I said:

'I've met someone.'

'Sorry, I lost you there. You're what?'

Once he understood, his face receded again.

'Right,' he said. 'I see.'

I thought he might end the call, but he only shook his head, incredulous. Met someone, he asked, as in *met* someone? A man, a Hesp, from Hesperus? Was I serious? Had I forgotten what I'd said myself, many times, about their backward attitudes towards women? Was I off the rails, was I having some kind of breakdown?

He raised both hands as if to calm me, or himself.

'You must be under a lot of stress,' he said. 'I get it, I really do.'

I broke the connection.

I searched my room for the lost key one last time, then retraced my steps to the library. I looked everywhere I could remember going on campus lately. Finally, it occurred to me to ask at the loans desk on the library's ground floor. The assistant was not interested, but she searched behind the counter, produced the key, and passed it over. No, she didn't know who had left it. She put her earbuds back in and turned away.

Troubled by a suspicion, I went up to the Special Collections room and pulled one of the crates off the shelf. I could tell before I lifted the lid that it was empty, and that the knotwork text of Fallon Herm's Red Song had been taken.

> • <

East Hesperus contained no sites of archaeological importance or more recent historical interest: only an expanse of housing blocks dwindling to shantytowns on the outskirts. I rode a public bus through Hesperus's chaotic traffic. I sat near the front, anxious not to miss my stop, and watched the driver taking calls on his mobile. Old cars with gouges along their doors overtook on both sides, lurched into every bit of space at junctions, and drove the wrong way down the bands of scree at the edges of the dual carriageway. It was oddly good-humoured. At home any driver cut up so often would have been incandescent, but this man braked equably through the near misses.

On the fifteenth floor of a high-rise block, I rapped on a fibreboard door. When Bron saw me he looked sheepish and led me into the flat. Kneeling on a bolster beside the low table, he unfolded a blanket to reveal Herm's knotwork, coiled for storage in the traditional manner.

He couldn't give it back, he told me. He did not seem to understand that we were both going to get into serious trouble.

'Fallon Herm didn't mean it to be locked in a storeroom. He meant it to be sung.'

Rain was spotting on the window and a watery Hesp sunset had spilled behind the city's mass of shadow. He folded the knotwork into its blanket and stood up.

'You persuaded me,' he said. He moved closer. 'I was losing my belief.'

'You can't keep the knotwork,' I said.

He went to put a pot of water on his electric ring. It had grown almost dark in the room, so I turned on a desk lamp that was standing on the floor. It threw a wedge of yellow light along the wall, and turned the dusk outside the window to darkness.

'I no longer believed the traditions could save us,' he said, a little later. 'But you spoke about Herm, and you took away my doubts.'

We were sitting side by side on the mattress that lay on the floor, resting our backs on the wall and eating stewed lentils.

'I'll have to report you,' I said.

He scraped the last spoonful from his bowl. I uncrossed my ankles and recrossed them. We were at opposite ends of the mattress: if I were to reach out, I thought, I could touch his shoulder with the fingertips of my left hand.

When we woke, an hour before dawn, Bron talked about Vada Cass. His elder brother had been imprisoned there for attending political meetings, and had disappeared in the massacre. Bron's mother had taken part in the subsequent street demonstrations and had died after being attacked by a soldier.

I lay beside him. The window brightened. After a while I sat up.

I said:

'I want to see it.'

> • <

We walked in the Old Town, passing from the Place of Shadows into the Green Lanes and over the Serpent Bridge.

Bron was silent. He moved briskly in spite of the holdall slung across his back. I was silent too. Each mask was kept in place by a large ceramic bead on a short piece of twine: the bead was held in the mouth, making speech impossible. At first I had been self-conscious about going out masked in public, but no one had given us a second look, and I soon found a sense of pleasant, potent anonymity. Witnessing a performance of Herm's text, however crude, would be invaluable to my research.

The bead in my mouth felt as big as a peach stone. It was smooth except for one rough point, a flaw in the glaze against which I was chafing my tongue. Our masks seemed to annul all questions of where we were going or why. We only walked.

Evening sun was reaching between the buildings by the time we came to the Place of the Songs. Fifteen masked people were already waiting there, and several more arrived as Bron set his holdall down, unfolded the blanket, and began to lay out the knotwork. Two or three others knelt silently to help him. When they had finished and the Song was spread on the flagstones like the skeleton of a huge fish, they detached a dozen strands from the tail-end. Masked figures moved forward to take them.

I joined the rest of the group as we formed a ring, facing inward towards the centre of the Place. I had lost track of Bron, and I could not pick him out in the circle of identical masks. Eyeholes watched.

The dozen holding the cantos of the Prelude had placed themselves at intervals around the circle. I watched one of them as she took the knots between her thumb and forefinger. She made no sound as she fed the cord slowly to her left.

Around the circle the same thing was happening, the cantos uncoiling as they made their way from hand to hand.

The recital took place in silence. It was dark before the cantos had passed around the circle and the Prelude was complete. In the glow of street lamps from beyond the rooftops, the gathering had become all the more anonymous. I could no longer tell who was male or female, who was young or old. We were pale masks hanging in the gloom.

A masked figure stepped forward into the circle. After a pause, a second figure did the same. I felt a shift in the atmosphere, as if a choice had been made.

Two more celebrants came forward, one carrying a jar and the other holding up two clay marbles, one black and the other white. The marbles were placed in the jar and the volunteers drew their lots. They looked into their cupped palms, neither showing what they had drawn.

One of the actors lowered his mask. I saw the mournful face of Olifer Tepp. He looked appalled at his position, and I wondered what had possessed him to step forward. He raised his clay ball to show that it was white. He was to be the antagonist, then. Figures gathered around him and took the mask from his hands.

The other actor displayed the black clay ball of the protagonist, and took off his mask. It was Bron. He looked calm enough, if a little disoriented. It must be strange to show your face to a crowd of hidden faces. He looked from mask to mask, and I had the idea that he was searching for me. Before I could be sure, others led him out of the arena to prepare for the role he was soon to play.

> • <

Overall, my six months in Hesperus were productive, and I came home with all the material I needed for my translation of the Nine Songs and the accompanying commentary. The book was finished by the end of the year and the first publisher on my list accepted it. When I think back on the fellowship now, I think of it as a turning point, instrumental in my landing a permanent post. To remind myself of this I keep my leather chorus mask in a prominent place on the bookshelves of my college office. Students like to ask about it, and I'll usually tell them some of the story. I wore the mask twice in the end. A full enactment of Herm's interpretation of the sacred drama was too valuable an opportunity to miss. Of course, some aspects of the Red Song are distressing in practice, but I felt it was incumbent on me not to judge. I was there simply to witness the playing out of Hesper's traditions. That I earned the trust of my hosts was shown, I like to think, by the fact that a package was left at the university for me on the day after the performance. It contained Herm's knotwork, skilfully reassembled and coiled for storage.

I may go back to Hesperus one day, but I have no current plans. Life is full. Seb tried to see me once or twice after I came home, but I did not have time for him. I am learning how busy life can become when your career takes off. How demanding and how rewarding. I am fulfilling my potential at last, and the possibilities seem endless. Some mornings I wake up and feel everything is new.

IN PHASES

I travel for my job. It's fine: three or four times a month I have to leave at short notice, but I'm never away for more than a night or two. Clare and I have not found it a problem, though things did get harder to manage after Felix came. At the time I'm thinking of he was four months old, and of course it killed me to be away from them. Plus I think Clare and I were embarrassed to be falling so easily into these roles, me going off to earn while she stayed at home with the baby. We felt like, could we really not do better? But the truth was that over those months I came to value my work trips in a new way. I'm not saying I didn't want to be at home every minute I could, but I did gain an appreciation for how simple and orderly life became when I got on the train, travelled to the assigned location, and did my work. Sometimes, too, I felt sure Clare was relieved when I left. I could understand why that might be, but every now and then I had a sensation like vertigo. As if I might fall away from them, and as if none of us would mind if I did.

I hardly know why I'm thinking of this particular journey. Nothing remarkable happened, but maybe that's the reason. Looking back now, I see we were at a point where things could have gone differently if our luck had not held. We were moving into a new phase of life, after all, and no transition is perfectly smooth.

Clare and I argued as I was leaving for the station that morning. It was 5.15 a.m., I was pulling on my clothes and she'd been up all night with Felix. He was going through a patch of bad sleep, the sort of normal developmental glitch that you forget as soon as it's over but feels like the end of the world in the small hours when the baby will not stop screaming, your wife is sobbing from exhaustion, and you have to bike to the station before dawn. I was already running late when we fought, over nothing really. I made some half-thought-through suggestion about how we might get him to sleep better, she curtly told me why it wouldn't work, I got defensive. Then I had to race to make my train and fell into the carriage out of breath, with the argument still loose in my mind. I wanted to make it up. I wanted to take the baby gently from her arms and support the weight of the hot, ribby, squirming little body. I would not feel easy until I saw the two of them again. But I knew she was glad to have me gone.

The rhythm of travel was soothing. Work claimed my attention. I put on one of the playlists of familiar songs that I find good for concentrating, and went through the file for the visit. For the first hour I had the carriage to myself except for a pink-haired young woman in a camouflage jacket, carrying a rucksack that must have weighed as much as she did. Our eyes met as she came down the aisle, and I thought I should help her lift the bag onto the rack, but by the time I was half out of my seat she had done it herself. For a few seconds I wanted to talk – to find out how she saw the world and to be understood in return – but naturally I did not bother her. Like any journey, this one was made of moments like that. Moments in which nothing happened, but which for all I know might have tipped some hidden balance in me.

The visit itself was unremarkable, practically textbook. The agency always books me into the same ubiquitous budget hotel chain, and I've come to like the way the corridors, bedrooms, check-in desks and bland breakfast areas are reproduced identically in hundreds of locations around the country. At least, I've come to appreciate it, the way you might appreciate a laboured joke. I took a taxi to the address. It was like any work trip: three o'clock in the afternoon, overcast, cold and getting dark, me paying the cab and peering at the numbers along a street in a provincial town, then pressing the buzzer of a bay-windowed terrace house that looked no different from its neighbours.

The appointments can be stressful in their way, of course. Emotions will be unstable, and the relatives tend to be confused about my role, often having unrealistic expectations of the assistance I can and cannot offer. Sometimes they even seem to believe that the agency I represent is in some way responsible for what has happened to them. As a rule, though, they are civil to the point of submissiveness, and they listen gratefully as I explain what they can expect from here on in.

I talked through the preliminaries and handed over some leaflets to the relatives, who in this case were parents in their early forties, both evidently suffering from a chronic lack of sleep, and an elder sister, perhaps twelve years old. I took them through the standard questionnaire, while at the other end of the living room the subject, indistinguishable from a three-year-old boy, played peaceably with a toy garage. No one had thought to turn the lights on, and I detected a kind of visual buzz, not quite a flicker, as if the dim air itself were a screen behind which a fluorescent light was malfunctioning. I caught a faint stink, too, like a single burning hair, and noted my impression that a film of grease had coated my hands and the inside of my mouth. Again, textbook. I'm attuned by now. The relatives did not seem to have noticed the feedback, and of course I did not point it out. Soon enough it would become impossible to ignore.

After securing the papers in my briefcase, I took time to discuss the parents' concerns. Everyone asks the same questions, and I've learned to make my answers simple. I'm honest, certainly, and I do not sugar-coat, but neither do I admit to ambiguities or gaps in knowledge. I do not indulge in sympathy. Today, as always, there were some misapprehensions that I had gently to correct. No, I told them, it's not him. No, I'm afraid it's not meaningful for you to ask where the real child has gone, or what's happening to him now. We simply do not know enough to give you an answer. (Here candour reaches the limits of its value.) I told them that the subject might carry on for months, years or decades giving every appearance of normality, at least to the casual eye. In that case, or in any other, the firm advice was to continue as though nothing had happened. Just pretend, I told them. I gave some advice on how to manage the symptoms of cognitive dissonance that they might expect to arise from this approach.

As I spoke, the father kept grinning as if to placate me, but I saw that the mother's response was going to take a different form. I was not surprised when she interrupted. It's another way of processing. Some people demand to be given all the available information, however technical, as if by grasping the facts well enough they might force them into meaning something else. Occasionally they can become confrontational, even accusatory – talking about conspiracies and cover-ups, or implying that I'm somehow personally complicit in their difficulty – and while I can understand such behaviour, I'll always make clear that it is not acceptable. This time there was no real problem. A little extra firmness was enough to calm the mother, and eventually both parents nodded their acceptance in the rather touching way I have come to recognise. They signed the release forms and promised to carry on as I had advised, doing their best never to discuss the matter, even between themselves, after today. To finish, I outlined the sources of support that they might consider drawing on – not many, regrettably, in spite of the increasing incidence. The parents took it all in. The daughter was bored. No one paid attention to the small figure playing or seeming to play at the other end of the room, which struck me as a hopeful sign for the future.

When I ended the visit it was after four o'clock and almost fully dark. I set off for the hotel in a state of guilty anticipation. The truth was that I could have travelled home that same night, but I had chosen not to. Instead, my plan was to eat a sandwich in my hotel room, finish off the paperwork at leisure, then read a little and watch TV for a while. Later, perhaps, I'd text Clare to see if she wanted to say hi before bed. I liked my work, I genuinely felt it made a difference, but I sometimes thought I enjoyed these moments most of all: the small intervals, the gaps between the claims of work and loved ones, in which for a few hours I had nothing to do and I could imagine that my life was neither one thing nor the other.

This time something curious happened. It was early evening, but as soon as I got into the room I lay down on the bed and fell into a shallow sleep. With some half-conscious part of my mind I seemed to be working out in great detail how I would travel home tomorrow, but I could not quite bring the train times, station names and platform numbers into focus as they reeled past. Then I found I was on the train and now my world ended at the ticket barriers, so that I would circulate forever in a purgatory of stalled coaches, seats musty with sweat, pungent toilets and station stops recurring like headaches. I scrambled up and went to the window, where I saw something monstrous in the darkness outside the hotel. It was a vast, cylindrical structure, prison-like, faintly luminous, almost invisible, crammed with the living bodies of the lost. Somewhere inside it was my son.

With an effort I gasped and blinked until I was awake, then washed my face at the sink. Hours had passed. It was almost ten o'clock. I was unnerved less by the dream than by the fact that I had fallen asleep at all. But after shaking off the disorientation, I felt better than I had felt all day. I was not tired. I said to myself: now you know what's real. I thought of Clare and Felix, and knew that I would do anything for them. For them, I told myself, I would sacrifice anything. I knew, in a way that I had not known when I left that morning, that life comes in phases and this is right and good. I could hardly believe I had been planning to stay away from home for longer than necessary.

Thinking of them safe and warm in our house, two hundred and ninety miles away, I looked up the train times and found that if I left now I could be there before dawn. I would step silently into the room and lie down beside them where they slept. None of us would need to wake up.

PILGRIM: HINTERLANDS

That January, Alex bought a gaming console. He did not know why. He had taken no interest in video games since he was a teenager, and now was not the time for a new hobby. Peter's father had had a stroke on Christmas Eve, and the past weeks had been consumed by grim phone calls, fatigued motorway driving and long waits in hospital corridors. The damage was serious. Peter was still going home whenever he could, but they had agreed that Alex could not keep going with him. Work had to get done.

In Alex's day, fifteen years ago, 64-bit had been state of the art. The new console was small and sleek, but the controller was exactly the futuristic instrument his younger self would have imagined: a bulbous form, bristling with buttons and pads, that looked awkward but turned out to fit intimately in the hands.

He made a mug of tea, powered up the console and entered the online store. He had a game in mind. For weeks now his browser had been showing him ads: a lone male figure in a windblown ankle-length coat, seen from behind, the set of his shoulders more exhausted than heroic, standing on a ridge and gazing down into desert and sky while a strange aircraft, a cross between a zeppelin and a paddle-steamer, sailed towards a city on the horizon. According to a review aggregator, the game was acclaimed for its huge open-world environment and its system of emergent mission design.

Peter would be away until tomorrow evening, so Alex bought the game and watched the download bar begin to fill. He had given up gaming at eighteen because it was so obviously damaging his attempts to have a life. It was odd to find that he could step back, at will, into this world that had been waiting for him. He swallowed a mouthful of tea, placed the mug on the floor, and rested his head on the back of the sofa.

When he woke it was dark outside and the room was ghastly in the glow of the screensaver graphics. He had been dreaming. Lately he had been having complicated dreams which seemed to carry over from one night into the next; he could never remember the specifics, only the sense that part of himself was living night after night through a weird, unending saga. Impressions of an endless journey, a flight from encroaching danger. He got up and closed the curtains. It was not yet midnight, but he felt rested, so he woke the console and started up *Pilgrim*.

Sixteen hours later, he heard Peter's key in the door and hurried to save his game. He stowed the console and controller in the drawer of the coffee table, then switched the TV to standby before stepping into the hall.

Peter was hanging up his coat. He looked at Alex.

'You're exhausted,' he said. 'Are you working too hard?'

'I didn't really get to bed last night,' Alex said.

'Idiot. Is it that bad?'

'Just trying to keep on top of things.'

'You'll make yourself ill.'

Alex nodded, penitent, while gameplay images flashed across the front of his brain. Tybalt running and diving for cover in a shantytown in the Edgewastes. Shooting it out with a rustler gang, making every headshot count. Taking on a ten-foot mutant barkeep armed with machete and knuckleduster. Leaping from the roof of a moving train to catch the rope trailing from an ironclad dirigible rising out of the Tar ravine. Gambling for salvation runes in the backstreets of Scorched River. Staggering through a burning whorehouse in search of the antidote to the venom of the white sidewinder. Hiding in the lee of a prehistoric totem, letting a fly crawl across his lips, while inches away the hunters of the Bone Crow sought his trail. Crashing through a window to rescue Alanna Daniels from a cannibal cult. Facing down a lynch mob with a single bullet left in the chamber of his six-shooter. Dying over and over to be reborn at the most recent save point. *Pilgrim* was a single-player 3D action-adventure-exploration-stealth-RPG of a type that, Alex gathered, was common nowadays, though to his younger self it would have seemed the unthinkable apotheosis of the hopes of every gamer. The player took the role of the cursed gunslinger Jem Tybalt, doomed to wander the earth without rest, who hid his melancholy beneath a taciturn exterior and whose duster coat rippled in the hot winds of the enormous, lawless continent known as the Hinterlands.

They microwaved leftovers while Peter brought him up-to-date on progress at home. There was none. It was five weeks now and his father still could not walk or form words, although he could sit up in bed and did seem to know familiar faces. His mother was not sleeping. The doctors were unclear about the prognosis, and Peter was doing his best to keep her from falling out with them. Alex nodded in comprehension, shook his head in sympathy.

When Peter went for a shower, he took the console out of the drawer and found a better place in one of the old file boxes in the office corner. Just before exiting the game, he had heard a rumour of an ancient codex that might have the power to free Tybalt from his curse. To learn the location of the book he must help Sally Dollar, the no-nonsense redheaded sheriff of Jawbone, defend her town from the troupe of bull-worshipping fanatics that rode in each spring to kidnap twenty-four youths and maidens for purposes too horrifying to dwell on. Of course Tybalt had agreed to the deal. That was how the game worked. He was forever fleeing, forever searching for some means of escape from the supernatural horror that pursued him (known only as the Tracer, it had the appearance of a tall thin man in a long black coat, though nothing human could follow so implacably). But his search was continually interrupted by other quests, which themselves opened into yet more challenges, so that the further Tybalt travelled, the longer his journey became. There was no doubt that finding the codex would be a gruelling and perilous task, nor that, once found, it would turn out to be only a single step on a far longer road to redemption. The progress meter on the menu screen stood at two per cent.

> • <

In the morning Alex lay and listened to Peter moving around the flat, boiling the kettle, flushing the toilet, calling goodbye. After the front door closed he stayed in bed, taking his time. He had been playing too much *Pilgrim*. Last night his dreams had swung and plunged around him like the game's environments, rich with threats to escape and tasks to accomplish. As usual, most of the details eluded him now that he was awake, but there had been another person in the dream: a slender girl with brown freckles and hazelnut eyes, who had told him their bodies and souls were in mortal danger from the thing that was pursuing them. He could not swear that she had not been there all along, that he had not been dreaming of her for months. They must never stop running, she had told him, slipping her small hand into his. He could still feel its warmth and smoothness.

He made coffee and settled himself in the office corner. Reports for three clients were due by the end of the week, but there was still time to get everything done. He would restrict himself to an hour of *Pilgrim*, he decided, at the end of the afternoon, just before Peter got home. The prospect would help him to work efficiently. But then again, he thought, scanning his emails, wanting to play would interfere with his focus. Maybe he should get his session with the game in right now, and free himself up for the rest of the day. He started up the console just before 10 a.m. At 6.30 p.m., with an effort of will, he shut it down. When Peter walked in twenty minutes later he was chopping vegetables for a stir fry.

That evening he put in a good ninety minutes on the first of the reports. He could meet his deadlines if he worked solidly for the next two days. Peter was in the kitchen, talking to his mother on the phone. The trouble with *Pilgrim*, Alex thought, was that it was so perfectly engineered to appeal to some basic, survivalist layer of the brain. You met one problem at a time and it was always life-or-death. Tybalt lived without hesitation, staking life and limb at every turn, and when he failed and died the game took you back to try again. You never ran out of lives, because the story had to continue. It made for a state of absorption in which hours passed unnoticed: a flow you just did not get in the real world.

The next day Tybalt's journey brought him to the mountain homestead of Serena Molloy, a hardscrabble frontierswoman who was also a powerful witch. She promised that she could protect Tybalt from the curse that afflicted him, and against his instincts he found himself drawn into a new kind of life, no longer on the run but playing the faithful partner as weeks and months passed. He worked Serena's land, protected her house and shared her bed, and perhaps (so his tired, easy stance suggested as he leaned on the fence-post he had been fixing in a cut-scene) found a kind of peace he had never expected. It could not last, of course, and it ended when bandits struck the homestead. Tybalt saw them off easily enough, but not before they had wrecked the circle of candles, runes and bones that Serena had constructed around the codex to activate its warding mojo. At once a familiar, sickening noise filled the homestead – a noise like the scrape of claws and the clink of spurs, the desert wind howling with a basso choral throb beneath, the sound of an approaching nightmare – and then the Tracer was there, closer than ever, its not-quite-human hands tearing down the planks of the door. Serena sacrificed her life to cast one final spell and hold off the demon long enough for Tybalt to get away. With her last words she told him to get to the city of Sweet Air and find someone named Evie Dylan, the only person who could help. Back on the road, alone again, Tybalt's face showed no flicker of emotion.

Alex had been planning to use the evening to make up the day's work, but as he was getting started Peter came home distraught. His mother had phoned. His father had started talking again, but in vile language, abusing those around him in hateful terms that he would never have dreamt of using before. She was in a terrible state about it.

Peter sat at the table and put his head in his hands.

'I need to go back,' he said, 'but I just can't. I've missed so much work already.'

Alex touched his shoulders.

'They'll cope,' he said, 'and if they don't, so what?'

Peter looked up. He had grey pouches under his eyes.

'This is more important,' Alex said.

They decided Peter should set off right away. He ate something while Alex packed him clean clothes.

'I wish I could help,' Alex said, handing him the bag and the car keys.

'You do more than you know.'

> • <

Alex sent emails to the three clients, offering sincere apologies that due to a family emergency the reports would be delayed. Tybalt was bushwhacked by slavers in a mountain pass and escaped with nothing but the clothes he stood up in, then had to track the gang to a remote ore-mining town to retrieve his weapons and equipment before resuming his journey towards Sweet Air. Shortly after 3 a.m., Alex got to bed and dreamed that Evie Dylan was the girl with the hazelnut eyes. She knew how to escape the thing that was pursuing them, and soon, she promised, she would tell him. The dream's atmosphere was reassuring and appalling at the same time. He was walking with Evie through an enormous open-air café in the ruins of a temple, but then they were in a squalid attic room high above a city, Evie cross-legged and naked, showing him where to touch her. When he woke he could remember every detail.

He showered, dressed, drank coffee, and started work. He had no desire to play *Pilgrim* today. He got an angry email from one of the clients and wrote a reply that was conciliatory but also, he felt, dignified in its insistence that some circumstances are beyond our control. He worked through to the evening, only pausing to check in with Peter. Peter's father now believed care staff and family members were his enemies. Alex got most of a report done. The only thing that nagged at him was the impression, which he could not shake, that as well as last night's dream he could now remember the dreams of the past several months, and they had all been a single story in which he and the girl called Evie Dylan had been travelling together, on the run through an endless landscape from the terrible entity that would never let them go free. He looked up a *Pilgrim* wiki, but could not find any reference to the Evie Dylan character.

That evening the late nights caught up with him and he fell asleep over a beer at the kitchen table. In his dream he was hand in hand with Evie, following her through alleys, plazas and arcades in the deserted city. Tears ran down his cheeks for the joy of this life in which they must never rest but must make their world of one another, must take their pleasure in one another and in the world even as they fled the damnation that followed at their heels. Evie, bare-armed in a beaded suede waistcoat, was explaining that the only way they could escape was by putting an end to themselves. If they did it right, they would be reborn into new lives and the devil would never be able to find them. She began to lead him down a long underground corridor, glancing lasciviously over her shoulder, and he understood that she was going to show him the secret, but then his phone was buzzing and he woke to Peter saying he was sorry for ringing so late but it was a nightmare, his father had said unforgivable things to his mother and slapped her in the face, and they were all just in pieces.

The lights were blazing, so Alex crossed the room and turned them off, revealing the kitchen as a formation of dark shapes. His senses were sharp. He could smell the stale dregs in the glass. Glowing numerals told him it was after two in the morning. Peter's voice grew tiny and indecipherable as Alex took the phone from his ear. He looked at the name on the screen, then hung up the call. He needed a moment's stillness, a moment for his mind to clear, because now he understood. Tybalt walking the Hinterlands. Peter suffering trials for which he had not been prepared. Evie promising that if we leave this world in the right way then in the next one we can be free. Alex held these pieces in his mind, letting them move into alignment, and as they joined he heard the front door open.

It was coming along the hall, its claws scraping the walls, its moan hollow and wordless beneath the clink of spurs. Alex smelled sawdust and hot iron. The air dried so suddenly that his lips tingled. He reached out to steady himself on the table, but his hand slipped and he fell. The phone was buzzing. He dragged himself across the floor, away from the approaching presence. Although he was terrified he was also filled with a vast relief. He wished he could speak to Peter. He would confess, tell him everything, and explain that it was all going to be okay. Listen, he would say. The further we travel, the longer our journey becomes. We live on the run from a curse but it is the curse that makes us free. We never run out of lives because the story has to continue. We do more than we know.

EURYDICE BOX

Eurydice Box wakes at half past six to find that her daughter has gone missing.

Daisy Box is five years old. Most nights they sleep in the same bed, and Daisy usually rouses Eurydice in the mornings by wriggling about under the duvet, wanting company in the waking world. This morning Eurydice is slow to surface. She spends a few drowsy minutes searching around in the bed before she understands that she is alone.

She finds her glasses, gets up and checks Daisy's room. She goes downstairs. Daisy is not in the house. Shortly before waking, Eurydice had a dream in which her own mother crept into the bedroom and took Daisy from the bed. It is hard to shake off the strands of this unreality. She pulls on a tracksuit top and calls Daisy's name. They are already running late.

Eurydice's phone lies on the kitchen counter with its notification light blinking. There are twenty-seven unread text messages and forty-four missed calls. All of these are from her mother. The most recent call was just before five o'clock this morning. Eurydice leaves the phone where it is. At present her mother is obsessed with Eurydice's decisions about how to live her life and care for Daisy, and for the past few days she has been bombarding Eurydice with accusations, ultimatums and demands. This is what happens when one of these phases is approaching its climax, and Eurydice knows that the best way to weather it is not to pay attention. At night she leaves the phone downstairs and on silent.

Now the screen lights up with another incoming call. Her mother. Eurydice goes back upstairs and looks into Daisy's room again, then into her own, as if Daisy might have been hiding under the duvet all along. Under the window the dual carriageway is thickening with traffic. The dread feels like a stomach bug. Eurydice touches her head to the windowpane. Then she flies downstairs, out of the small house that her mother calls their matchbox, and along the row to the corner where Daisy has just come into view. Daisy is barefoot, wearing only her pyjamas. Frost glints in the fissures of the tarmac path. Eurydice scoops her up and carries her indoors.

Sitting on the kitchen stool and having her feet sponged, Daisy is unable to explain what she was doing. She cannot say whether she managed to open the door for herself or whether she found it open. She does not seem to know why she went outside.

'I stayed on the pavement,' she says.

They are well behind schedule now, so Eurydice manhandles Daisy into her uniform and gives her a bowl of cereal. Eurydice gets dressed and comes back downstairs to see her phone lit by a call. This is the worst possible time for it, but for exactly that reason – because she is shaken or her resistance is worn down, or because in this moment she wants the conflict – she answers.

There is silence on the line for several seconds. Then:

'Eurydice. *Darling.*'

Her mother does not sound surprised at getting through. She pronounces her words very slowly and emphatically, as if she has been asked to give a performance of languorous poise and make it as broad as she can. Eurydice, holding the phone between her ear and her shoulder while she brushes Daisy's teeth and pulls her into her coat, asks her mother what she wants.

'Want?'

Her mother's tone is one of baffled and wounded innocence.

'What do I *want*?'

Eurydice zips up Daisy's coat and fastens her shoes. She has forgotten to make a packed lunch. On the line, her mother sighs operatically.

'She can only think of what people want from her. It must be my fault, I suppose.'

'It's a bad time,' Eurydice says.

'A bad time,' her mother says. 'A bad time.' She is tasting the words, slowing them right down. 'When was it ever *not* a bad time, for you?'

Eurydice makes a jam sandwich and puts it in the lunchbox with two digestive biscuits and the browning half-apple that is the only fruit she can find. She fits Daisy's bicycle helmet and fastens the strap, lifting Daisy's chin so as not to pinch the flesh underneath. Her mother is talking about how all she has ever done is give and give and give, and how all she wants in the world is a little ordinary human kindness from her daughter and not to be systematically and sadistically denied contact with her only grandchild.

'As it happens, I've been consulting my solicitor,' her mother says. 'He informs me that it's eminently possible for a grandparent to win sole custody of a child in cases where the mother is incapable of caring adequately for that child.'

'I have to go.'

'Oh, that's right,' says her mother, and now they have reached the point at which the affectations crumble and the raw hostility comes through. Eurydice ends the call and hustles Daisy out of the house.

Eurydice has a heavy iron bicycle that she thinks of as Dutch. It has a plastic crate on the front and a seat on the back for which Daisy will soon be too big. The ride to school takes fifty minutes. As Eurydice pedals along beside a stream of traffic, a man in a navy blue suit gets out of a parked Jaguar, throwing the door open in her path. She slews to avoid a collision, and a four-by-four blows its horn. She is waiting at the traffic lights when the same vehicle stops beside her. A middle-aged woman lowers the window to berate her for cycling so stupidly, and with a child on the bike as well. Eurydice does not look at the woman. She waits for the lights to change, panting, knowing they are going to be very late for school and that the secretary will show no sympathy as she makes Eurydice sign the list.

> • <

Eurydice Box is gangly, with elbows and knees that she feels are too big for her frame. Her face is small-chinned and long-nosed, as if it was drawn out a little too far by the hand that moulded it. Her large thick glasses sometimes seem to get between her and the world. She wears eight-holed oxblood boots, dayglo leggings and a man's battered leather jacket with a sheepskin collar. Under her bike helmet, her hair is restrained by a red bandanna with white spots.

Eurydice stands outside the school gates and checks in for work. The app on her phone registers her location, searches briefly, and comes up with the first gig of the morning. The app tells her how long a visit is expected to take – sixteen minutes, in this case – but she has to accept the assignment before it will tell her where to go. It is entirely up to her whether she takes any given visit, but if she declines too many her rating will fall and her hourly rate will slip down the scale. The same thing will happen if she takes longer over a visit than the app allows. All of this has been made clear in the terms and conditions Eurydice accepted when she signed up. She takes the gig, swings a leg over the bicycle, and pedals away from the school.

There have not been any more calls from her mother. Perhaps this morning's conversation was enough for now.

By the time she reaches the address, she has eight minutes left to carry out the visit. She spends three of these waiting to be buzzed up to the flat. The client is a man in his eighties, frail and apparently living alone, who seems confused about who she is and frightened by her sudden arrival. He smells of excrement. She introduces herself brightly and briskly from behind her face-mask while she pulls on a pair of latex gloves from her backpack. All supplies are meant to be provided by the clients, but this never happens so Eurydice buys her own.

She guides him into the bathroom. There is not enough time to help him with a full shower, so she removes his trousers and underpants, gets him to hold on to the sink, and cleans around his private parts with soap and a flannel. He endures this without complaint. His face in the mirror is rigid with anxiety. There is not much Eurydice can do to reassure him. She has just under a minute left, which is enough to finish up and sign off the visit on schedule. If she can accept the next one ahead of time, her rating will go up a fraction.

As she is dressing the client, he begins to soil himself. Foul-smelling greenish liquid runs down his legs. He cannot move to the lavatory, so she lays toilet paper around his feet and leaves him where he is until the accident is finished. She puts on the cagoule that she carries in her backpack, then undresses him, helps him into the bathtub, and washes him under the shower. She cleans the floor with more toilet paper, a hand towel and the dregs of a bottle of bleach. By the time the client is dried and dressed and she has finished rinsing out the soiled things, she is almost twenty minutes behind and her phone is chiming to warn her of the damage to her rating. She takes the stairs of the apartment block three at a time, accepting the next gig as she goes.

She spends the next five hours biking around the city on the route the app determines for her, trying to make up the time she has lost. It is always like this, one way or the other – she always ends up racing – but today the late start means she does not stand a chance. Some of the clients she has seen before and others are new to her. Most live alone, and many suffer from cognitive or psychological problems along with their physical impairments. When she cannot persuade them to open the door, she has to tap *visit failed*.

Twenty minutes before she is due to collect Daisy from school, she is trying to soothe an elderly woman who initially mistook Eurydice for her own daughter and has become agitated on discovering her mistake. Finally, Eurydice leaves the woman's house, takes out her phone and ends her day's work. She's managed four fewer visits than she should have in the time, and her rating will suffer accordingly. School pick-up is in ten minutes. She checks the map and finds that she is a strenuous half-hour's ride away from the school.

She is sweating and out of breath when she presses the button beside the school's automatic gate. After a pause, the intercom buzzes and the gate begins to open. The car park is mostly empty. She expects to find Daisy sitting on the chair beside the secretary's office, and she is ready to submit to a lecture about how persistent problem lateness at pick-up places an unacceptable strain on school resources and raises child protection flags. This time, Eurydice thinks, there'll be a meeting with the principal. But Daisy is not on the chair, and when Eurydice knocks at the office door the secretary's look, though puzzled, is no more contemptuous than usual.

'Daisy was collected by her grandmother today,' the secretary says, interrupting Eurydice's explanations. 'Were you not aware of this?'

Eurydice bounces the heel of her hand off her forehead, laughs at herself.

'Sorry, of course, yes,' she says. 'Just got mixed up for a minute. You know.'

The secretary does not know. Her expression is doubtful. She stares, impervious to apologies and thanks, as Eurydice backs out of the office.

Miranda Box-Haughton's house is a double-fronted Edwardian mansion that stands on a hill in a green suburb to the south of the city. The house is surrounded on all sides by its garden. The garden is enclosed by a limestone wall which is topped by a dense hedge. This is where Eurydice grew up.

Eurydice lets her bike fall on the gravel. She thumbs the doorbell for a good ten seconds, hearing the brassy peal in the hallway. She thumbs it again. She tries Miranda's phone, but gets no answer there either. She walks around the house, looking through the windows into the big, dim, tidy rooms.

Miranda is in the conservatory. She is dressed in her Katherine Hepburn style: a silk blouse and high-waisted, wide-legged slacks. She holds secateurs in one hand and a spray bottle in the other, and she is drifting among the tables of geraniums and tomato plants with dreamy slowness. When Eurydice taps on the glass, Miranda sets down her tools one by one and admires their placement before coming over to the French doors. She walks with her deportment-lesson gait, treading along an invisible tightrope and swaying her hands rhythmically in front of her hips. She wears an abstracted smile.

'Where's Daisy?' Eurydice says.

Miranda looks reproachful.

'Nice to see you too, darling.'

Eurydice knows only one way to manage these encounters. Her face is stony. She will not raise her voice or show irritation. She will not argue or engage. She walks past Miranda and through the conservatory.

There are eighteen rooms in the house, not counting corridors and cupboards. Eurydice has not been here much in recent years, but everything is so familiar that she is immediately at a disadvantage. Objects seem more than solid. Scale and distance deceive. Even the light falls oddly, skewed by the decades through which it has to pass. Miranda follows her through the rooms, amused. There is no sign of Daisy.

'Did you pick her up or not?'

Miranda puts on a playful face: maybe I did and maybe I didn't. Rather than respond, Eurydice goes into the front hall. Here she finds Daisy's school bag with her school uniform piled on top of it, neatly folded. Miranda stands at the foot of the stairs with one hand resting on the newel post and her head thrown back as if she is posing for a photograph.

'You need to tell me where Daisy is.'

Miranda laughs musically.

'Eurydice, darling, you're *storming* around.'

Eurydice feels she might break her rule now, and start saying everything there is to say. This would only make things worse.

'I simply dropped by to see my only grandchild coming out of school,' Miranda says. 'And it was lucky I did, since you didn't trouble yourself to turn up. Poor Daisy's teacher was *very* glad to deliver her into my care. Any other mother would expect gratitude, but I know better.'

'Where is she?'

Miranda rolls her eyes.

'Darling, this is dreadfully dull.'

Eurydice pushes doors open, calling Daisy's name. Miranda giggles.

'If you must know, she's gone on a little day trip with Roland.'

Eurydice's fear stills and centres itself. It presses at the base of her skull.

'The dear fellow was terribly keen to spend some time with her, one on one,' Miranda says. 'He really thinks of her as his own child, you know. And the poor girl so desperately needs a positive male influence in her life, don't you think?'

'You need to tell me where Daisy is right now,' Eurydice says. Her voice sounds ugly in her ears. This is how it works, every time: she ends up sounding like a bad soap opera.

'Oh, yes,' Miranda is saying. 'Because you care *so* much.'

When Daisy was three, Eurydice was visited by social services. Someone had reported that she was keeping her daughter in an environment unsafe for a child. They would not give the details of the accusation, or tell her who had made it, but when Eurydice brought it up with her mother a look of naughty glee spread over Miranda's face. She has the same look now.

'What are you going to do, then?' Miranda says. 'Since you always know best.'

Eurydice draws a breath. The air in the house is cold.

'You've let a stranger take my daughter,' she says. 'You need to tell me where they are.'

Miranda presses a hand to her breastbone and gives a tinkle of laughter.

'It's awful to see you like this. Flailing.'

Eurydice only half hears as her mother tells her that she's not fooling anyone, she doesn't give a damn about Daisy because if she did she wouldn't keep her in that squalid house and make her live that squalid life. She doesn't deserve to keep Daisy if she can't take care of her. She probably wants to be rid of her anyway.

'That's it, isn't it?' Miranda says. 'You just *wish* something would happen to her.'

Eurydice says nothing. Roland Starling is the latest in her mother's procession of boyfriends or consorts. Most of them stay for a few months, some for a couple of years. They move into the house. Miranda declares each time that she has found the love of her life and gets offended when Eurydice fails to be impressed. Starling has been around for ten weeks, and Eurydice has met him once. She remembers the striped old school tie that he wore, the old-fashioned MG coupé that he drove and the wetness of his lips when he insisted on kissing her cheek. Besides this she knows nothing about him.

This is all to Miranda's purpose, of course. The idea is that now Eurydice must give up her stoniness. She is meant to start reasoning and negotiating and persuading. She is meant to listen to whatever her mother wants to say.

'Have you any idea how hurtful it is when you describe my Roland as a *stranger*?' Miranda says. 'Have you any idea how much you've hurt him by refusing to let him make a relationship with our grandchild?'

Eurydice opens her mouth to reply. Then she turns away from her mother and leaves the house through the conservatory. She collects her bike and wheels it down the driveway, unsteady on the gravel. Miranda has opened the front door and is shouting something, but Eurydice does not look around. When she reaches the street she puts on her helmet, mounts the bike and cycles away.

She is almost at the corner when her mother's dark blue Alfa Romeo snarls past and brakes hard. The window slides down.

'You've shocked me before,' Miranda says. Her eyes are dark with hatred. 'But this is something else.'

Eurydice does not move. She has one toe on the road, balancing.

'If you care, they've gone to White Meadows. It happens to be a place that holds fond childhood memories for Roland and he wanted very much to share them with his granddaughter.'

Eurydice gets out her phone and checks the location. A nature reserve on the river.

'One day I won't help you,' Miranda says. 'One day she'll find out what you're *really* like.'

The car revs and accelerates away. Eurydice rides on until she is a safe distance from the house. She dismounts and leans against a wall. As soon as she stops shaking she will go in search of her child.

> • <

The only vehicle parked by the entrance to the White Meadows nature reserve is an old-fashioned MG coupé. Eurydice leaves her bike by the fence and passes through the kissing gate. Right now she and Daisy ought to be eating beans on toast and watching a cartoon. The reserve did not look big on the map, but now Eurydice is walking into an unfolding green maze between banks of nettles and brambles that block all lines of sight. In the dusk she cannot tell how deep the trees go or where the pathways lead. She walks quickly, straining her eyes and ears.

The paths branch and merge, peter out and return. There is no knowing which is the right way. Every angled branch and receding thicket is a suggestion. Beyond a stretch of rough grassland she finds the river, screened by undergrowth and dead trees. The surface of the water is almost still, but Eurydice can see it flowing deep and fast underneath.

A gap in the bushes shows a muddy slope. Two people are standing at the water's edge. Roland Starling holds a small garland of wild flowers and grass. Daisy is in some kind of frothy white gown. Her bare toes poke out below the hem. As Eurydice watches, Starling sets the garland on Daisy's head. He steps back to admire the effect, clasps his hands to his mouth and lets out a small sob of emotion.

Before Eurydice can move or speak, Daisy catches sight of her and runs over. She gives her usual greeting after they have been apart for any length of time, throwing her arms around her mother's waist, lifting both feet off the ground and digging her sharp little chin into Eurydice's stomach. Eurydice takes the twisted grass ring off Daisy's head and lifts her up. Daisy locks her legs around her and immediately starts rocking back and forth in her mother's arms as if she's bored.

Starling stands in front of them, absurd as a waxwork. His moustache is dyed the same unnatural black as the wedges of hair above his ears. He is dressed in a striped shirt, a blazer and an old school tie, but his trouser legs are rolled up to the shins and his bare feet are covered in mud. Eurydice thinks he must have looked just like this at boarding school when one of his masters caught him doing something disgusting.

'Look here,' he says, and Eurydice realises he is on the verge of tears. 'I think there's been a mistake.'

He takes a step closer and Eurydice draws back, gathering Daisy more tightly in her arms. Starling tries to laugh, but it is the laughter of a condemned man.

'I was given to understand…'

He pauses and shakes his head, unable to find the next words. Eurydice keeps her eyes on him as she feels her way back up the slope, but with Daisy in her arms she cannot move fast enough to prevent him from blocking their way.

'I'm terribly sorry,' he says. He is cross now. He seems exasperated by the position in which he has been placed.

He reaches into the pocket of his blazer and takes out a folding knife. It is large and tarnished. Eurydice imagines him using it for woodcraft and boy-scouting, hacking his initials into fence-posts in his miserable youth. He shows it to her with a kind of apologetic defiance. This is dashed awkward, his manner says, but a chap's got to stand up for himself, hasn't he? A chap's got to insist on what's right.

As he is opening the blade, he fumbles so that the knife snaps shut and springs out of his hands. It disappears among the nettles and long grass. He goes after it, falling to his knees to grope where it landed.

Eurydice sets Daisy down, then strides over to Starling and kicks him as hard as she can. She has not hit anyone since she was a child. She is surprised by the force of which she is now capable, and by the damage that can apparently be done when an eight-holed oxblood boot connects with a man's naked ankle bone. She hears a pop and feels something give. Starling howls and collapses onto his side.

Eurydice carries Daisy out of the nature reserve. Her foot hurts. They hear Starling sobbing behind them, calling for help and cursing all the women who persecute him so unfathomably. The evening is peaceful, not so cold now as it was earlier in the day. Daisy lets Eurydice strap her into the bike seat, and lifts her chin willingly to have her helmet fastened

> • <

They get home an hour after Daisy's bedtime. Eurydice leans her bike against the lamppost outside the house, holding it steady with her hip while she unstraps Daisy and lifts her out of the seat. Daisy is tired out and clings groggily around Eurydice's neck. Eurydice locks up the bike and opens the front door.

While the bath is running, she takes Daisy out of the white dress and bins it. She locks both locks on the front door. She sets her phone to silent, then turns it off. Daisy loves the bath and has woken up a bit at the prospect. She leans over the tub to watch the bubbles rise. Eurydice dips a hand into the water, then adds more cold and mixes it around.

Eurydice washes Daisy. She starts at her feet, using a flannel to rub off the remains of the mud. It tints the water a little as it dissipates. Daisy's body is frog-legged, pot-bellied, no-necked, double-chinned, and staggeringly beautiful. There are no marks on her skin. She closes her eyes and tips her head back so that Eurydice can wet her hair. When they have rinsed out the shampoo, Daisy pretends to be a fish, twisting onto her belly and slipping up and down the bathtub. She gets excited and slops a lot of water over the floor and Eurydice's clothes. Eurydice loses her temper, shouts at Daisy and lifts her out of the tub. Daisy gets upset, but settles down when Eurydice wraps her in a towel and holds her on her lap.

They put on their pyjamas. Daisy watches a cartoon while Eurydice finds something for them to eat. They have peanut butter sandwiches and Daisy has a chocolate yoghurt. When she starts to fall asleep at the table, Eurydice takes the spoon from her hand and scrapes off the yoghurt that has dripped on her pyjama top. She picks Daisy up and holds her one-handed to brush her teeth and clean her face with the flannel.

As Eurydice lays her in bed, Daisy stirs and says she wants a story. She is barely awake. Eurydice turns out the light. She gets into the bed, fitting herself around Daisy's curled spine and working her thumb into Daisy's warm palm. She sings their first song. They always sing the same songs in the same order. Eurydice often drifts off while singing and is woken by Daisy demanding the rest, but tonight Daisy passes out almost at once. She twitches, mumbles and settles.

Eurydice sings more quietly, then stops. She is tired but not sleepy. She should go downstairs and get ready for what comes next, but she does not move. Daisy is usually a restless sleeper, and most nights she ends up sprawled across the bed, all feet and elbows. Eurydice does not want to waste the chance to lie with her like this, warm and close, with no space between them.

THE MONSTROSITY IN LOVE

Amy Semper was twenty-two years old. Her hair was cropped short and dyed black. She wore gunmetal eyeshadow and heavy kohl. One of her ears was pierced in five places, the other in three. Her style of dress suggested the art-school dropout: camo jacket, rara skirt, sixteen-hole boots. She had a white umbrella patterned with red strawberries, and the way she twirled it on her shoulder, like all her gestures, said that the hungry gazes and clumsy overtures to which the world subjected her counted for nothing, because she pleased herself.

We met in June 2019, on a street in Shoreditch, just after two o'clock in the morning. She was walking away from a sobbing young man, and caught my eye conspiratorially as she passed. Soon I learned that her living arrangements were fluid. She moved from one shared flat to the next every couple of months, invariably falling out with each new set of flatmates before long. Most nights she stayed over with a boyfriend or a conquest, but sometimes she would stay with me. She knew she could come over when she was sick of the drama she got from everyone else. She would press the intercom in the small hours and I would buzz her up. I'd put on Davis or Coltrane and sit in my dressing gown while she moved around the room, pouring herself a glass of claret, browsing through my books. Finally, she might settle cross-legged at the other end of the sofa, in the soft light of the Tiffany lamp, and tell me: Nicholas, you look terrible.

Speak for yourself, you old bat, I might say. Or perhaps: my dear, I *am* terrible. Then we would sit together until dawn, Amy smoking and drinking, me listening to the music, neither of us saying very much. She might tell me about some project she had taken on: a singing or modelling job, perhaps, or a part-time gig in a café or a gallery. I would respond with the requisite lazy irony, and we'd decide that it was a waste of her talents, not worth seeing through. At other times she would vent her annoyance with whichever unwise young person had most recently decided to fall in love with her. She liked my line in weary incredulity that anyone could make such an absurd mistake. If I got hungry, she would lift her cigarette permissively as I left the flat. Coming back an hour or two later, I would find her curled on the sofa, sound asleep.

We saw one another two or three times a month for those first few years. Once, during a peaceful evening making fun of her latest ex, we were disturbed by five men wearing Kevlar armour, carrying electroshock rifles and steel spears tipped with hawthorn stakes. They smashed in my front door with a battering ram and invaded the flat in tight military formation. One of them survived long enough to tell me, with his own combat knife pressed to his throat, that he had been seeking revenge for what I had done, some months previously, to someone he had loved. I did not doubt that the grievance was justified, though I could not recall the specific occasion he was talking about.

After laying the man out beside his associates, I set aside my irritation and turned to Amy. I thought she might be rattled, but she stretched her legs along the sofa and took up the conversation where we had left it. That was the trouble with love, she said. Everyone thought it was good, but it was the root of everything that was stupid and wrong.

'When you're *in love*, you value one person above the whole world. Above life itself. That's what they always tell me. And they congratulate themselves for it. They think it's a good thing.'

'Monstrous,' I said, licking the back of my hand.

'It's hypocrisy.'

She nodded at what was left of the intruders.

'If I ever tell you I'm in love,' she said, 'you know what you have to do.'

> • <

Not long afterwards I gave Amy a key to the flat. I had never done this before, but it seemed a natural step. I saw no reason why she should not come and go as she pleased, and for a year or two we continued much as ever. Now and then I would wake up to find her on my balcony, watching the sun set between the blocks of Banister House. I would lean beside her to gaze out over Hackney. From four floors up, the people struggling along the streets looked like what they truly were: reasonably detailed dolls, distinguished from one another by unimportant variations in appearance and in the problems of their brief lives.

When neither of us was attending to other affairs, she would stay all night and we would continue the conversation we had been having, in our desultory way, ever since we met. One night I rummaged in the bureau and showed her a battered silver ring. I'd had it since I was eighteen, I explained. The woman who gave it to me had been at least ten years older.

Amy slipped the ring on and admired her hand, then looked more closely at the words engraved in the metal.

'It's Latin,' I said. '*Love conquers all.*'

'And did it?'

We laughed. Amy thought the ring quite suited her, so I told her to keep it. I never saw her wearing it afterwards.

Another night the horizon flickered prettily – this was late in 2025, and the North London culture riots were entering their third week – but Amy seemed less interested than usual in passing comment on the scene below. There was a new ingredient in her psychic scent, a note unfamiliar to me. After she left I wandered around the flat for a while, eventually throwing myself on the sofa with a copy of *Thérèse Desqueyroux* I had bought in Marseille in 1929 and had never got round to reading. But I could not concentrate, and a few minutes later I was coursing through the city, my substance spread thin to merge with darkness. I searched, tasting the night, and caught her trail south of the river. I coalesced in the shadows to see her leaving a franchise pizza restaurant hand in hand with a gangly, balding man. She stood on tiptoe to kiss him before they parted.

I let her find her way to an ill-lit, deserted street, then slid close and put my mouth to her ear.

'Who was that old geezer?'

Amy gasped. Then she slapped my arm.

'He's the same age as me, smart-arse,' she said. 'His name's Robert.'

'I like his anorak.'

It turned out that Amy had been seeing him since the summer without telling me. He was an inventor. I stifled a snort. He had his own startup company, and he was developing a fully biodegradable alternative to high-density polyethylene.

'It's going to do so much good,' she said. 'Why are you laughing?'

I shook my head.

'Shut up,' she said, and elbowed me. 'He's nice.'

As if that was not enough, this Robert had persuaded her to go back to college and finish her A levels. I pretended to be horrified that she would consider such a dreary idea, but she looked at me as if she thought I really cared one way or the other.

'I have to do something, Nick,' she said. 'We can't all be twenty-five forever.'

> • ⟨

By the time she married Robert we had fallen completely out of touch. When I thought of her it was to reprimand myself for making an exception. I told myself I should have known better than to get attached, however slightly; I should have known that for all her bravado she would turn out like the rest.

She and her family lived in an attractive townhouse in one of the gated compounds of Telegraph Hill. Once or twice I made my way there and hung on the wind in the darkness outside. I saw her in the lit windows, a woman in her mid-forties putting three children to bed, tidying the kitchen, having a glass of wine with her husband, doing some paperwork. These days she worked in fundraising for a charity that aimed to alleviate mental health problems arising from social isolation and loneliness.

I began to find my preoccupation a little vexing. We had not spoken in fifteen years, but I still saw things I wanted to draw to her attention, as if to make a point in some argument we had left unfinished. When the hunt led me into a slum indistinguishable from the slums of Gladstone's time, with the same starved faces and the same messages of hatred scrawled on the walls; when my phone invited me to enjoy my access to the democratic process by taking part in yet another digital plebiscite on a vital issue of the nation's future; when I rested in some high place three hours before dawn and watched the indentured workers disembarking from lorries with private contractors' logos on the sides; when the outraged young staged a joyous protest against war or capital or injustice or whatever was felt currently to be the problem: at such times, more often than not, I thought of her. Look, I wanted to say, haven't you noticed your mistake?

It was a distraction, and eventually I decided something had to be done.

Amy was not a good sleeper. Late one night she went down to her kitchen and turned on the lamp. She did not seem surprised to see me. As she pulled her dressing gown around herself, I saw how much she had changed: how heavy her body was now, and how creased and swollen her face. Her grey-blond hair stood in tufts.

I got up, watching to make sure that she understood why I was here. But even as her eyes hardened, I found myself smiling apologetically, raising my hands and retreating as if it had only been a joke.

I swept through the rain and the darkness, embarrassed. I had thought massacring Amy's family would end my difficulty – would make my point and put her out of my thoughts for good – but evidently the opposite was true. I could not work out why, but face to face with her I had seen that making them my victims would be tantamount to admitting I had lost the argument.

It was all trivial in any case, I decided. I had grown set in my ways and narrow in my concerns. That night I made travel arrangements, and in the years that followed I treated myself to a nostalgic grand tour. I revisited the landscapes I remembered from a journey I had made around Europe in the spring and summer of 1767. I sought out my favourite statues, paintings, chapels and dark alleys. Then I travelled to other places where, at various times, I had formed fond associations: Tripoli, Jerusalem, Guayaquil, Santiago, Yangon, Nairobi, Hobart, Svalbard. I passed a civil evening in Vancouver with the small, dapper man who had sired me in the Walks of Gray's Inn one night during Michaelmas Term of 1623. In Budapest, I helped some brothers and sisters put down an outbreak of lycanthropy, and became embroiled for a time in the paranoid politics of clans, packs and covens. When that grew dull I moved on and spent an unmeasured period drifting eastward, keeping to sparsely populated areas, forgetting speech and thought, seldom separating myself from the darkness, driven by appetite alone. That ended when I found myself a prisoner in a Tokyo facility dedicated to the containment, analysis and weaponization of the likes of me. Those were tiresome years, but they concluded with a pleasingly eventful escape in which my jailers learned the colour of their kidneys and several researchers came fully to understand the inadequacy of their world-view to the reality they had chosen to confront. As I expanded from the underground corridors into fresh night air, I felt an inclination for home.

❯ • ❮

I stood on the balcony of my flat and watched the sun setting over Hackney. The skyline had not changed in my absence, which was curious: this was not the first time I had returned to an old haunt after decades away, and on previous occasions I had generally come back to find that a town of wood had become one of brick, or that an unremarkable riverside settlement had sprouted skyscrapers, or that the palaces of the aristocracy were burnt-out shells. But now I found myself looking down on the streets and roofs of half a lifetime ago and finding them perfectly familiar, as if the world had no more changes to offer.

The air inside the flat should have been stale from long vacancy, but it was evident that someone had been here a matter of days ago. I breathed deeper, tasting the scent. I knew it, but it was different from before. She would be sixty-eight years old now.

I stayed away from the flat for a week or so, and came back to find the trace renewed. I lay on the sofa for a while, brooding on what would happen if I stayed until her next visit, but a sort of shyness came over me at the idea. Instead, I turned on the Tiffany lamp, set a glass beside a bottle of claret, and put *Autumn Leaves* softly on repeat. Then I went out into the night.

The following week, the flat was dark and silent and the bottle was empty. A silver ring lay on the table. I picked it up and read the engraved words: *omnia vincit amor.* I slid it onto the smallest finger of my left hand, and nine days later, when a key scraped at the door and Amy Semper let herself in, I was waiting.

She put her handbag and overcoat on a chair and took her usual place at the end of the sofa. Instead of folding her feet underneath her in the old way, she sat down slowly, stiff-backed, clasping her hands in her lap. She wore a smart suit and her hair was cut in a feathery crop that made her features more prominent than I remembered. I poured her a glass of claret.

'You look well,' I said.

For a moment I thought I had offended her – this was not a type of conversation in which I'd had much practice lately – but she only nodded.

Robert had died of a heart complaint four years previously, she told me. It had been unexpected. She was living alone now, in the house on Telegraph Hill, and she was still working full-time with no plans for retirement. She felt that her work was more important than ever. Mental health problems, from depression to the new memory disorders, were epidemic on a scale that had been unthinkable at the beginning of her career. She was frankly baffled by this new trend for claiming there was something political about it, as if illness could be a form of protest.

I listened, not saying much, as she got into her stride. She spoke about climate genocide and antibiotic resistance and catastrophic migration and the rent war and the erosion of representative government. I wondered if she realised how much she seemed to care about everything these days, but I kept listening as she told me how her children all lived far away and how none of them were particularly interested or grateful. Her eldest daughter had not spoken to her since Robert's funeral, and she had a grandson whom she had only met twice.

Eventually a different expression passed over her face – a flickering smile that made her look, briefly, twenty-two again – and she held out her glass for a refill.

'Stuff on my mind,' she said.

That was why she had started coming to my flat. It was a good place to clear her head, she explained, away from everything. She shot me a sidelong glance, and again I saw that she was the same person she had always been. There was something unpleasant, almost monstrous, in the idea that my Amy was still in there. Perhaps inside herself she did not feel so different from the young woman who had caught my eye at two o'clock one morning, forty-six years ago. A chill prickled my scalp and I had an urge to get away from her as fast as I could.

She drained her glass and I passed her the bottle.

'How've you been, anyway?'

'You know,' I said. 'Same.'

She filled the glass, and I pictured her in the lit windows of the house where her family had abandoned her. I pictured her drinking wine, tidying her kitchen, doing her paperwork, checking the news, worrying over all the things she cared about. I pictured her cleaning herself in the glare of a big bathroom, climbing stiffly into bed and reaching to turn out the light. Pity was not my thing, and it had never been a good look for Amy either, but as we sat there I came to a decision. I would make it easy for her. I would not make her come out and admit that I had been right all along.

I moved along the sofa towards her.

'The sooner we do it, the better,' I said.

She blinked at me, her eyes cloudy and her lips wet with the wine.

'It'll hurt, but not for long.'

She hardly seemed to know what I was talking about. Then her eyes focused and she was on her feet. Her glass bounced and a dark red stain began to spread on my Kashan rug. She was staring at me as if I had made some unspeakable proposition, and I heard a petulant note in my voice as I asked what I had been supposed to think when she turned up at my flat in the dead of night after all this time.

She snatched up her handbag, fumbled with the catch, and took out a hawthorn stake. It was almost a foot long, sharpened to a knife-point. It shook in her hand in the space between us.

'Amy,' I said, calmly now. 'What do you expect to be able to do with that?'

She sat down, put the stake on the coffee table and took a couple of deep breaths, finding her composure.

'Nothing,' she said. 'Unless you want me to.'

We talked a good deal more before I understood what she had thought was happening between us. That she truly believed time had proved her right, and that in her mind I was the one trapped in an existence from which I must long for release. In her version of events, this was why she had come back to me.

'How many has it been, Nicholas?' she said at last. 'How many over the years?'

I gave her a blameless smile; a let's-not-be-vulgar smile.

'How many what?'

She glared, doing her best to be angry, but she could not keep it up. Her eyes crinkled and her mouth curled, and she was the Amy I knew, the Amy with whom I was complicit in all possible mischief, the Amy who understood that to take the world seriously was an unpardonable lapse in style.

She stepped out onto the balcony for a minute, as if she wanted fresh air or the glow of the night. When she came back in, she lay down on the sofa and I settled myself on the floor beside her. I leaned back so that our heads touched, and in that position, half dozing and half awake, we kept each other company until dawn. We did not say much, but now and then one of us would think of something and murmur a reminder of the old times, or of our old selves, the way we used to be.

WE HAVE BEEN TO A MARVELLOUS PARTY

To begin with you are going on a holiday with your family. Your children are young, younger perhaps than you would have expected, the youngest small enough to ride in a pushchair. At a service station some older children loiter near your picnic table and one of them tries to impress his friends by harassing your loved ones. He offers sexual insults to your wife. In an ideal world you would grasp him by the neck, force him over to the kiosk and batter his face relentlessly into the plate glass. This being impracticable, you pretend that what is happening is not happening. You are a clown of propriety, peremptory and stiff, chivvying your family away from the scene as if they are to blame.

In due course it becomes apparent that you and your father are standing naked and washing yourselves in an open shower area that has been installed at one end of a large, busy room. Colleagues and acquaintances go about their business. You know better than anyone how he suffers but you cannot make it easier. He will never speak of what has hurt him in his life. Instead you fall into a guilty row with your mother over one of the outrageous statements she makes as if they are common knowledge. She has claimed that people can be divided into the strong and the weak. Your indignation is excessive and you are losing the high ground. You throw a china cup at the tiles. Now that you have started you cannot stop.

Next comes the celebration you have been promised. It is not clear how the children are accounted for but it does not seem to be a concern. The beat pounds through all the dark chambers of a labyrinthine structure, a honeycomb of shabby rooms. The two of you have come here together and you cannot find anyone you know. She has taken a pill so music flows through her and she dances with superb strength and grace. The party's half-light reveals it all with the most attentive intimacy. She is too old to be acting this way yet by virtue of this very fact she has never been younger. The beauty she has now she could not have had at twenty, because she had no need then to demonstrate such gallantry, such valour, such nerve. You stare in at her where she dances, safe with her delight. You were supposed to take the pill but you were scared and chose to pretend. She does not seem to care that you are a traitor. Her face is ablaze and she keeps coming back for you, reaching out. You have known one another such a long time and you would do it all again.

An interlude now in which you have been banished to a haunted house that is a universe in itself. There are no windows or exterior doors, only a series of dusty, junk-filled rooms lit by bare bulbs in brass stands. You have arrived with four strangers but the evil spirit of the house incites an orgy of suicide and murder and soon you are the only one left. Over the weeks that pass, as you try to devise a means of exit, you come to understand that you have been in this place before. You were brought here as a small child and languished alone for an ageless lifetime before being released to reality. As you recover the memory you begin to tear at the boarded-over fireplace, bloodying your fingers, kicking the planks away. You find a shaft extending horizontally for hundreds of metres, its roof so low that you would have to wriggle on your belly to investigate where it leads. From a hatch at the far end an organism unfolds with gloating languor. A dead spider with orang-utan limbs and the head of a maths master. Little sharp-toothed helpers swerve like tops towards you and you do not have time to turn away.

What follows is an afterwards with the family taking occupation of a kind of cabin or chalet, a small timber house of modernistic design and inept construction. Uncurtained picture windows overlook wet pine forest in all directions. You set your luggage on the warped floorboards. It is not what you were led to expect. You drove up miles of mud track to get here and it will be impossible to get the car back down the way you came. The artefacts of the previous residents are everywhere: foreign-language magazines, unfinished woodwork projects, photographs of irrelevant teenagers, folding knives. Directly you are in the middle of your meltdown, hysterical with self-pity and fear. Your children do their best to calm you. Your older boy is developing a suite of tics and stereotypes before your eyes while the other two are learning to be silent, to give way and accept defeat. Even as you inflict the harm you are seeking excuses for your behaviour. You imply that this is a private crisis, the sort that can be resolved merely by coming to terms with the fact that one day you are going to die. At that your wife cannot help laughing, and after a moment you join in.

Soon enough you all feel better. You unpack and take stock of the board games. You make dinner. You joke a little about the padlocked door at the end of the hall. You wonder what it will be like in here when the daylight goes.

SEAFRONT GOTHIC

Off season and not a soul on the promenade. Shuttered ice cream parlours, chains on turnstiles, arcade machines frilling their lights for no one. Driving all day makes things less than real. The hotel was out on its own, a shabby hulk with unlit windows, and as I tried the door I was already telling myself I had wasted a journey.

The young man standing at the check-in desk was watching me, glassy-eyed and rigid, as if I had dropped a coin in a slot to have my fortune told. He looked capable of standing like that forever. But at length a smile stiffened his face.

'Hiya, Tobes,' he said. 'Welcome to the Seafront Gothic.'

> • <

I woke to the screaming of gulls and a splattered skylight. Niall had put me at the top of the hotel in a room barely wide enough for the single bed. I threw off a sheet speckled with black mould, dressed and found my way down to the dining room. The tables were set but no one was around. I lifted a fork: it was coated with dust.

'There he is,' Niall said, behind me. 'Have a seat, wherever you can find one.'

He disappeared through a swing door before I could answer. He had a knack for getting me tongue-tied.

I had tracked him down through mutual acquaintances – not that there were many of those. None of his friends had seen him, but I heard from someone that he had left the city.

Finally, one of his old girlfriends had given me the name of this place.

Niall returned with a tray and set out my breakfast.

'Enjoy,' he said, and whisked away.

White specks rotated on the surface of the liquid in the teacup. On the plate lay two strips of grey fat, two carbonised triangles and a clump of pale matter, jelly in the middle and burned around the edges.

I found him in the lobby, behind the desk, pretending to scribble in a notebook. He looked up, blank-faced.

'Can I help you?'

Two elderly men were sitting in a pair of armchairs. The lenses of their spectacles matched the lobby's windows: opaque with smears, scratches, dust. One of the men lifted an enormous grey handkerchief to his mouth and convulsed in silence. Niall put down his pencil and walked away.

'What are you doing here?'

I followed him down the corridor and into the bar room, where as I entered I had the impression that two figures were leaving by separate doors. Then I saw a mirror on the wall and understood that one of the figures had been the reflection of the other. Niall reappeared behind the bar and began to wipe it down with a cloth.

I said:

'It's about Allie.'

> • <

She was the youngest of us, and naturally we were protective. I was, at least. Niall pretended not to have any feelings of that kind, and it was true he had never been as close with her as I was, but I knew he cared in his way. I knew that when he understood the situation he would put rivalry aside.

I had been worried about her for a long time now. For years she had been drifting away: she seldom answered her phone, her replies to my emails were terse if they came at all, and once when I called at her flat unannounced she looked almost frightened to see me. She stood in the entrance with the door half-closed. I knew something was going on, and I was not surprised when, the next time I phoned, she admitted a man was making her life difficult. His name was Sol. It was the first I had heard of him. The situation was hard to explain, she said.

With a sick feeling in my chest I asked whether he had hurt or threatened her, whether she was in danger, where she was right now. I told her to leave at once and come straight to my place, or that I'd fetch her if she preferred, but she laughed and told me not to worry. I'm fine, she said. It's not like that. We just can't be in touch for a while, all right?

When you've always been someone's big brother, it doesn't feel right to leave her to fend for herself, but Allie had her own life. I told myself that if she needed help she would let me know, but after several weeks of silence I decided it could not go on. Her safety outweighed other considerations, so I went back to her flat. If this Sol was there and he wanted to make trouble, so be it. I had a right to visit my sister.

The door to her flat was answered by a woman I had never seen before. She told me she had been living there for three weeks, and she didn't know where the previous tenant had gone. Perplexed, I tried Allie's phone, but it rang out. The second time it went straight to voicemail.

I was seriously concerned. Allie might be hard to reach sometimes, but it was not like her to vanish. I sought out everyone she knew, however slightly, but none could tell me anything. I had been asking around her friends for almost a month when she phoned from a withheld number and told me we needed to meet.

We both arrived early at the place she had named, the café of an arthouse cinema on the other side of the city. I knew what she was going to say: things had gone bad with Sol, and she had moved to get away from him. She needed to be where he couldn't find her. Can you imagine it? Seeing the girl you've known since her infancy sitting at an aluminium table, an adult, worn by her life, hurting in ways you cannot help or understand. She had kept her overcoat on and put her bag on the floor. She wore her hair in a loose ponytail. There were fine creases at the corners of her eyes and mouth. I reached for her hand in a reflex of affection. I had never noticed them before, those creases, and they made me feel, as sharply as ever, that I did not yet know her completely: that there would always be more to discover. I felt as if we were children again, a boy of thirteen years and a girl of eight.

She withdrew her hand and told me she had come to a decision. She was moving away for good, and this time not just south of the river but to another hemisphere. She wasn't going to tell me anything more about her plans; she had to feel sure that no one could trace her. I begged her to see sense, arguing that she couldn't let herself be terrorised. I got angry, thinking about this faceless criminal who had invaded her life. He mustn't win, I told her. Men like that must not be allowed to win. I don't know what he's done, but you mustn't run away. We'll protect you, I said. We'll teach him a lesson.

When I ran out of steam I was glaring at her across the table, breathing hard, and I knew her mind was made up.

> • <

I walked along the promenade, the wind going through my shirt. My patience with Niall was running out. I had told him everything and he had acted as if it was not his concern. A woman watched me from the entrance of a shop. She wore a sheaf of necklaces decorated with metal discs like tiny coins. Her shop window contained bits of hippy junk: dreamcatchers, incense burners, crystal balls, pewter goblins. I nodded a greeting as I passed, but she stared back as if she had never seen such a gesture before.

Back at the hotel I noticed that all four of my car's tyres were flat. Three boys, ten or eleven years old, were sitting on the concrete wall, watching me with big grins on their faces. A mongrel nosed at their feet, then danced on its hind legs to try and grab something that one of the boys was holding out of its reach. The boy threw the object into the air, and the dog leaped and caught it. It was a stone: I heard the teeth clack.

I climbed stairs and walked along corridors. At the top of the hotel, I found an open door. The room was the same size and shape as the one I had slept in last night. In front of a cathode-ray television set a Sega Mega Drive nestled in its own wires. A big silver portable stereo with two built-in speakers stood at the foot of the bed, and cassette tapes were stacked in crazy towers against the wall. The cassettes were home-copied, like the ones we used to make, with the album titles and track listings written on the inlay cards in ballpoint. Looking closer, I saw they were the ones we had made. Many were in my own handwriting.

I looked out of the window. Across an angle of the roof, I saw the heads and upper bodies of two people talking in front of the hotel. One was Niall. The other had her back to me, but the curve of her hair and shoulder gave me an idea I could not ignore. I pressed my forehead to the glass, then ran down a flight of stairs and found another window on a landing.

Here I could see that the young woman was not Allie, after all. Of course not. In profile she was really nothing like my sister. She was a rather unfortunate-looking woman, in fact, who at best resembled Allie got up in a grotesque disguise. She squinted through thick spectacles. Her hair was dry and ratty, and she wore canvas overalls that Allie would never have considered.

I carried on down to the lobby, intending to catch Niall, but when I reached the front of the hotel he and the young woman were gone. The only people in sight were a mature couple, his hair silver, hers brass, walking on the seafront in matching vermilion shell-suits. They stared at me, astonished, until I went back inside.

> • <

I found Niall lying on his side in the empty fireplace of the dining room, with one arm up the chimney. His face was smutted with soot. The unfortunate-looking woman was standing over him. She turned away from me, dragging her hair across her face.

'Hello,' I said, noting again how unlike Allie she was. Her nose was a lumpy snub. Her hand repeated the fitful movement through her hair, and she hurried past me, almost breaking into a run as she left the room.

Niall scowled.

'Was that necessary?'

He was trying to sidetrack me again, but I was not going to allow it.

'We need to leave,' I told him.

A clot of soot fell into his face.

'What are you supposed to be, anyway?' I said. 'The caretaker?'

He wiped his face with his free hand, smearing streaks across his forehead.

'If you like,' he said.

He gave a cry of triumph and pulled his arm free of the chimney.

'Here, hold this.'

The object he passed me weighed nothing, and smelled of nothing. It was a dead magpie. I swore and dropped it.

'There's more, I guarantee you,' Niall said.

He began to thread his arm back up the chimney, then paused and sat up in the hearth. His arm was black to the shoulder.

'You know she isn't going anywhere,' he said.

I was holding my hands away from my body like a scrubbed-up surgeon.

'I told you,' I said. 'She's got no choice.'

Niall shook his head. He was no longer smiling, but there was a kind of affection in his face.

'Look, Tobes. I'll say this much. There is no such person as Sol.'

All at once I pitied him. Something had gone wrong in his life, I realised: there must be a reason he had decided to make a bad joke of himself. I spoke as gently as I could.

'You're not making sense,' I said. 'Why would she tell me those things?'

Niall was settling back into the fireplace, reaching up the chimney again. Already the honest look had been replaced by a smirk.

> • <

I leaned on the promenade railing and watched the water, trying to get the fresh air through my head. The waves were small but violent, the water dark even where it was shallow. The waves had a gel quality in spite of their quickness; where they ran over rocks it was hard to see where the water ended and the rocks began.

I had spent an hour walking around the side-streets, trying to find a tyre pump for the car. Eventually I had remembered my roadside assistance scheme and trailed along the seafront in search of a phone signal. With the sea to my left and the hotel behind me, I walked to where the town began to run out; or I thought I did, but I must have got turned around, because when I looked up I found the hotel was ahead of me again, though the sea was still on my left. I tried a pay phone outside an ice cream parlour, but the handset was dead. Now it was getting dark.

I knew Niall's smirk. I could unfold his whole fantasy. It was ridiculous to insinuate that Allie would invent the story of Sol; ridiculous that she would pretend to be abandoning her life. It showed a nastiness in Niall that surprised me, even now. He wanted me to think the worst of her and of myself. His lie had tiny hooks to it, but they were not getting into me.

I turned away from the rail and looked up at the Seafront Gothic. In the failing light the hotel seemed larger but less substantial: a print on wet sky. Light showed in an attic window.

A figure was coming along the promenade. I knew it well. I knew her proportions, the way she held her head, the way she placed one foot in front of the other, the unstudied pendulum swing that made the simple action of her walking not just fascinating but nourishing to watch. There was no mistaking her. Not trying to explain it to myself, I hurried forward, and I saw what should have been obvious all along, though it had seemed too irrational to consider. If she looked like Allie in disguise, this was because it *was* a disguise: I saw the falsity of the teeth, the cheapness of the wig, the joke-shop distortion of the oversized spectacles, the rubbery pallor of the putty on her nose. I didn't care why she had done it. I only wanted to embrace her.

When she saw me, she turned back the way she had come.

I followed. She picked up her pace and I did the same. I called out her name, but she did not stop. Instead she ran and I ran after her. Without intending it I was in full pursuit, hearing her quick breathing and her feet slapping on the paving slabs. I asked her to stop, pleading with her not to be afraid. Another voice was shouting too, somewhere above me, but now she had come to a place where a flight of steps led down to the strand. She took them dangerously fast, stumbled at the bottom and kept running towards the sea. The tide was halfway out and the beach was a treacherous landscape of shingle, mud, rocks draped in seaweed and drifts of plastic. She fell, but picked herself up before I could reach her. I slipped, cracked my knee on a rock, and hauled myself forward.

A voice called my name. Niall was leaping down the steps. I ignored him and kept going, because her ankle had turned on a rock and she had fallen full-length. When I caught up, she was sitting in wet sand. I dropped to my knees beside her and tried to catch my breath. The tide was out but the waves sounded close. She pushed the hair out of her face.

She was not Allie. Her features were not a disguise: she was a different person, with even less resemblance to my sister than I had thought to begin with. I mumbled an apology. She was gripping her ankle with both hands. Niall reached us and she let him help her back to the promenade, where, I now saw, other people had lined up along the railing. The woman with the coin necklaces was there, and the boys, and the couple, and others.

With the locals helping the young woman to limp away along the promenade, Niall came back. My knee was already too stiff to bend. He got me upright. We walked up the beach and climbed the steps.

As we started back towards the hotel I tried to say something, but I was oddly short of breath. Most of the sea was shadowed but the horizon was a rod of bright silver. I leaned on Niall and he held me steady. He touched my shoulder as if to say that as long as I was here, I need not worry about making myself understood.

DANGEROUS HOUSE

Once I tried to run away. I hid supplies in what we called the summerhouse, a rotten shed filled with junk at the bottom of the garden, then woke early one morning and crept out. It was the first thing I learned about myself.

My plan was to go and hide in the dangerous house. No one would find me there. After collecting my supplies I climbed through the broken panel in the garden fence. I knew the way. I had no friends but I was good at ranging around by myself. I knew holes through fences and railings and shortcuts across patches of woodland. I knew little-used footpaths, and the old railway line that you could walk along, a dirt track between tall brick walls under trees. My dad and I called it the abandoned line.

My dad ranged with me when I let him. He liked putting off what he was meant to be doing and squatting at my level instead. He would get more enthused about my projects than I was: exploring the garden, say, or making a suit of cardboard armour. I associated him with a particular flavour of embarrassment.

For my mother, another flavour. In her mind she was an exile from the life she should have had. Somewhere in history she had been betrayed and now she was stranded here. She once had a migraine that lasted two full weeks, during which Dad and I hovered outside the darkened room, dimly aware that her suffering was beyond what we could understand.

There was no one else to speak of. A girl called Jean once adopted me as a kind of pet, but one day I took off my shoe and used it to hit her in the face. Her nose bled and she shrieked less from pain than pure affront. That's how childhood is. Your own actions are things that happen to you.

The dangerous house had a sign. *Dangerous House: Do Not Enter.* I wanted to live in it, behind the broken panes, in the shadows of rooms, with big holes in the roof to show sky through the top-floor windows. I wanted to be a thing that could live there.

When I reached the house that morning I saw it would not work. The upper windows showed the sky but I could not see a way to enter. The dangerous house was not a house. I went home and was back in bed before they woke. I had always thought of the town as being made up of the houses where people lived, but also of places where you might want to live but never really could: the green steel sarcophagi in the electrical substation, or clusters of crumbling yellow chimney pots, or the safe dark spaces under the iron grilles of pavement drains.

That is a kind of wanting my parents would not have admitted. It is not clear what they did want for me. I may have disappointed them, but I cannot be sure because I cannot see myself from the outside. I do not know what I am like, though I have picked up the odd clue over the years. I am humourless but I fail to take life seriously. I cannot seem to give people what they expect. I have a degree because I belong to this generation and social class, but my mother thinks I chose my job specifically to disappoint her. I have no ambition. I do not know what ambition would mean. I seem to be waiting for something.

My thought then is that I am waiting for the day when I can go and live in the dangerous house. I do not know yet what that would mean. But when I think of it, I think of an event that happened in the town when I was small. It had nothing to do with me. I only learned it as an item of gossip, overheard, but it settled in my memory. Somewhere in the town, the story went, a young boy had been lured into a derelict house by a pair of older children, twins, a male and a female. The house had once been part of the National Children's Home. I had never been near it because I knew of no way through the high steel fences. The story did not reveal what the twins had done to the boy inside the house, except that in the end they had taken him into an attic and left him there, bolting the trapdoor behind them. This happened on a hot afternoon in the middle of August. When he was found, the boy was unconscious and dehydrated. Questioned, the twins freely admitted what they had done, but could not be made to see anything wrong with it. There is no more to the story. The boy was okay in the end, if that's what you mean by okay.

But I think of him when I think of the dangerous house. Think of the boy in the attic, stifling with the stored heat. He is alone now in the unfamiliar space, its dark crossed by needles of dust and light, trying to breathe, not calling out, only waiting and not knowing, as he waits, whether for him there is meaning left in the word *wait*, for all that the air moves through gaps and that through the gaps he can still hear the noises of a summer afternoon: insects and traffic and a strimmer cutting down grass not so very far away.

BLOODYBONES JONES

I had not seen Rufus for three years, but when he appeared on the doorstep wanting shelter for the night, I was not surprised. He's my brother.

Up in the flat, he dropped his whole weight into the sofa. He surveyed the fitted bookshelves, the framed posters from Latitude and Electric Picnic, the screen prints Gwen's sister had made for us, the coffee table we had found one Saturday in the antique shop on the corner. His skewed canine tooth caught on his lower lip in the way it did. He let his grin widen.

'You would not believe,' he said, 'how hungry I am.'

I did not reply. Every move at this stage was crucial, and a false one could mean disaster. I walked into the kitchen, but when I came back with some cold pasta bake he was asleep, snoring, with his head rolled back and one boot resting on the coffee table. The leather was peeling away from the steel toecap.

I sat down opposite. He had changed his look. His hair was long now, hanging loose and greasy around his face. He had a cut on his cheek and his army surplus greatcoat stank of cigarette smoke. I wanted to remove the boots and the coat, clean the wound and cover him with a blanket, then grab him by the ears and shake him until he confessed why he had come.

Instead, I turned out the light and went to bed, treading carefully so as not to disturb Gwen. She had been having trouble sleeping since the start of the third trimester, and was liable to wake at small disturbances, but as I eased into bed she did not stir. If he was still here in the morning, we'd deal with it, I thought. I lay awake for a long time, but at last I dreamed I was in the back garden of our childhood home with someone who was both Gwen and Rufus. The garden was evil and would only let us go if I could perform a certain magic trick with a coin, but Rufus or Gwen kept laughing and pointing out how I was getting it wrong. I woke to find I had slept through the alarm for the first time in years.

Gwen was leaning on the kitchen counter with her crutches beside her. Rufus, bare-chested under the smelly coat, pushed the plunger of the cafetière. Adhesive sutures had been applied to the cut on his face. Usually I would have gone to Gwen and pressed a hand on her stomach to feel the strong movements of limbs under the surface, but instead I gestured lamely towards my brother.

'He's going to stay as long as he needs to,' Gwen said. 'You promise, don't you, Rufus?'

Rufus pressed his palms together, prayer-wise, and bowed.

Leaving them was against my better judgement, but I was running late. As I kissed Gwen's cheek in the hall, I restrained myself from telling her not to listen to him. I only told her to take it easy. The pelvic girdle pain she had been suffering since the middle of the pregnancy had eventually forced her to begin her leave early, and she was under orders to rest up. I reminded her daily not to try and walk. Joining the queue at the bus stop, I shook my head in admiration at the instinct that had made Rufus choose now, of all times, to make an appearance.

Our most recent encounter with him had been the day before we got married. He had arrived without warning, having ignored my previous attempts to contact him about the wedding. At that time his persona was based loosely on jazz-age hedonism: he was wearing two-tone shoes, hair oil and a charity shop pinstripe suit, complete with a fedora, and he insisted on taking us for whiskey cocktails and talking in brittle aphorisms. He kept on calling Gwen 'kid' and toasting us in an exaggerated way, as if he thought approving our union was his business. We changed the programme so that he could give one of the readings, but at the ceremony he was nowhere to be found.

And now she was meant to be avoiding strain. I spent the day not phoning her, knowing I could not afford to show concern. When I got home it was to the smell of cooking and the sight of Rufus wearing my blue-and-white apron, lifting the enamelled casserole pot out of the oven. Gwen poured two glasses of Malbec and a blackcurrant juice for herself. Rufus had spent the day going from market to market, it turned out, gathering his ingredients. He was picky.

'You didn't have to,' I said.

He paused, letting that statement hang, cocking his head as if to catch all its echoes. He chuckled to himself. Earlier, Gwen told me, she had taken a long hot bath at Rufus's suggestion, and had spent the rest of the afternoon in a completely pain-free nap. The baby was kicking.

As Rufus stirred the pot, making spiced steam rise, he explained that it was a simple dish, the trick being in how he used the tomatoes, lemon and garlic, but that you had to find good meat, as well, which was less easy than you'd think. He had picked up the recipe in Spain. He had worked for three months as a security guard in a Bilbao shopping centre last year, chasing shoplifting kids down the hidden access corridors behind the arcades. You could collar them but you had no legal right to detain them, so it was a question of what you could get away with. Usually he'd end up sitting on some angry boy's chest for forty-five minutes until the cops turned up, or else they didn't and the kid went back out to pilfer some more.

He had shaved since the morning, leaving himself a long moustache and a pointed piratical chin-beard. His towel-dried hair was caught back with a rubber band. He wore one of my T-shirts, stretched tight under his armpits, and a pair of my old jeans, showing inches of hairy shin below the cuff. As we ate, he continued on the theme of his recent employments. You never need to worry about money, he said. If you want some, you find yourself a job and you work until you have enough. Then you leave. Before Bilbao he had picked apples in Belgium. Further back, he'd been a runner for a reality television production company in Mexico City, he'd driven cars coast to coast in the USA three times over, he'd worked his passage from Nova Scotia to Oslo on a container ship, he'd been a waiter in a gourmet hamburger bar in Dublin. I gave as little encouragement as I could, but he needed none. When he got bored with somewhere, he told us, he was out. Next train. Why wait? If you let yourself get tied down, you might have a comfortable existence but you weren't truly alive. Of course, a lot of people would have trouble with his philosophy. But Rufus didn't need a label to tell him who he was.

I was watching for any flicker of mockery, but his eyes were fixed on Gwen. He poured himself more wine and pointed at her with the bottle.

'Live in the moment,' he said. 'Travel light.'

He raised an eyebrow.

I chewed a mouthful of the stew. The meat was so overcooked that it might have been anything. I pictured Rufus catching pigeons, wringing their necks and stuffing them into his greatcoat's pockets.

'I've got work tomorrow,' I said, as soon as I credibly could, but when I made to rise from the table he caught my forearm and gripped it with long yellow fingernails. He took Gwen's forearm in his other hand. He looked into her face, then into mine, slow and steady.

'You two,' he said. 'You guys.'

Before letting us go, I realised, he was going to give us his blessing.

'I want to say one thing, you guys, and I hope you'll remember it down all the happy, happy years ahead.'

He shook his head, smiling sentimentally. I waited, but instead of fading the smile stayed and grew broader, splitting to display teeth. His eyes showed white all the way around. He held his face in its rictus until I pulled my arm free and walked out of the kitchen.

'Night then, mate,' he called.

> • <

Gwen was breathing steadily beside me when I heard a noise: a tapping, soft but rhythmic. I slipped out of bed, crossed to the window, and opened the curtain. A big white face grinned at me through the glass. Then the grin was replaced by a look of cartoon surprise, and the face disappeared. The bedside clock said 1.38 a.m. The flat is on the first floor, and when we went down we found Rufus lying among smashed herb-pots on the paving stones of the back garden. He had climbed out of the kitchen and somehow edged around the corner of the building to our bedroom window.

'I'm so broken,' he mumbled, but in fact he did not seem to have done himself serious damage. He giggled. Gwen knelt beside him and tried to make him keep still, but he was already rolling around and getting to his feet. Half an hour later she was sitting in front of him in the kitchen, cleaning his grazes, watching for signs of concussion and carefully not asking what he had been trying to do. I went back to bed.

In the morning he was sprawled across the sofa, sound asleep under his coat. His face was peaceful.

'He's having a hard time,' she said, breathing into her tea so that her glasses misted. 'I got him talking.'

I opened my mouth. Then I closed it again, marvelling at his knack of blocking my every move. Gwen was explaining the kind of hard time that Rufus was supposed to be having. She thought he needed help. He kept checking the doors and windows.

'In the end, he told me he was scared of someone he called Jones. Any idea?'

I shook my head. I pressed a palm to my temple, which was throbbing with the lost sleep, and went to work.

I knew I should not be leaving her with a man who was demonstrably a danger to himself, if not to others. But there was no choice, because if I stayed at home it would mean he was calling the tune. I must give no credit to his impersonation of someone who was not responsible for his own actions. I could not blame Gwen for being sympathetic, or for imagining he did not know what he was doing when he pressed his face against our window.

It was only decent of her, but I could not afford to be so indulgent.

At work the day passed slowly. I thought about Bloodybones Jones. I saw what he was up to, of course. It had not been an important or lasting presence in our childhood, but just important enough, perhaps, for a tiny doubt. Could it be that a forgotten children's game, trivial then and meaningless now, could have affected Rufus so deeply that it was returning as a personality disorder? I knew the answer, but I had to admit he had chosen well, because the doubt was possible, or it would have been for someone not on his guard.

There were three years between us. As a child, Rufus had been small and credulous, unable to resist being hauled and shoved where I wanted him, and always ready to believe what he was told. He had spent his childhood beset by fears he could not explain, and hemmed in by all the places he would not go because of the menace that lived there: the compost heap, the turn in the stairs, the boiler cupboard, the wardrobe in the spare room, the attic. If I encouraged him, it was not out of malice. There was a kind of tenderness in the way I taught my brother that something would reach a hand out of the cupboard and grab him as he scurried through the hall, and that it was sending him messages in the knocking of the central heating pipes at half past five in the morning. I do not know which of us gave the thing a name, but it added to the fun. Rufus plucked at his hair, chewed his fingertips and broke things. He stamped on the toys he loved best. I understood why. He did it when Bloodybones got too close, because a sacrifice could keep it off a little longer. Of course, I know now that a twinge of guilt might be in order, but it was nothing unusual, as things go between brothers, and didn't Rufus get his own back in time? The summer when he was fifteen, he grew into his adult height and breadth. We no longer went in much for physical tussling by then, but he found an occasion for it, and I was held face down in the scrubby ground behind the house until I was gasping to breathe and there was no missing the fact that I could not get free. He never laid a finger on me again.

> • <

On the bus home I thought again of sending Gwen a message, but I left my phone alone. I had made it this far without letting him score that particular point. Send him on his way without putting yourself in the wrong, I told myself. He had come back to get something, as he always did, but what he wanted he did not deserve and could not have. And actually it was that simple, I saw. I got off the bus and started walking.

The flat's outer door had been left wide open to the street. Puzzled, I stepped in and eased it shut. The door gave into a cramped vestibule from which a flight of stairs ran up to the flat proper. I listened, straining into the still air of the five rooms. As I began to climb the stairs, treading like an intruder, a picture formed in my mind, and by the time I reached the landing it seemed really possible that I had made an error of judgement. Past events fell into a pattern of signs that had been plain for me to read. I saw the meat Rufus had served us, the grinning face at the window, the broken toys and Bloodybones tapping its codes on the pipes.

The living room was tidy and deserted. I moved into the kitchen, weighing the odds as I opened the door that Rufus would be waiting here in the blue-and-white apron, as two-dimensional as a nightmare, standing over the remains, red-handed, ready to explain that everything was all right now. But the kitchen was empty. I was alone in the flat.

Locking the street door behind me, I walked, remembering that in last night's dream Rufus had been in a kitchen preparing a meal with the assistance of some unidentified person. I had craned and jostled to see what they were making, but Rufus and the other had kept their backs to me and I could not push between them. I turned onto the high street and hurried along, scanning faces. The evening was cold and dull, losing light. A breeze lifted river-smell from a hidden source. I hesitated in the glow of the Metro supermarket and saw them.

They were walking towards me, Gwen using her crutches and Rufus escorting her tactfully, hands ready to give support. Their pace was unhurried. Seeing them, you would have taken them for a happy pregnant couple returning from a stroll around the block. When they noticed me, they smiled.

LISTEN

Voices spread in waves down these corridors. I hear the sobs of lunatics. They bring me to a room, strip me naked and drench me with cold water. The water smells of bleach and stings my eyes. Fingers force my mouth open and a steel tool probes my teeth. I have lost my diary. A light blinds one eye and then the other. My private parts are appraised by the hands of a fishmonger. I am made to swallow medicine and dress in someone else's clothes. I am sent along corridors into the vast cold rooms where the mad people are kept.

My brother comes to visit with an autumn morning clinging to his overcoat. Sunlight brightens the wall. He grasps me by the back of the skull and gazes into my eyes. He is looking for me where I am not to be found. Those who live in the world must believe that a human being is a surface concealing a depth, that a human life is a sequence of changes and continuities experienced in strict order by a named subject. I would help him if I could. I would teach him that we are long dead and that we have not yet been born. But he must live in the world and he will never be free.

Two boys go walking with their father to a pond where they plan to bathe. The pond is in a great park that is set in a great town. To the brothers the park appears to be an endless wilderness. Hemmed in by tall banks and tall trees and by tall houses that rise behind the trees, the water is as wide as a great lake, stretching away so that its far shore is folded behind banks and reeds and grasses and trees and cannot be seen. The sky is a solid glaring grey. Nothing moves.

The boys are too frightened to swim. They beg their father not to swim but the father is determined. He takes off his clothes and strides to the water. He wades to his knees, his waist, his chest, without hesitation, and then strikes out with competent strokes. His head moves across the water, drawing a wake that spreads in waves to touch the shore at the brothers' feet. They stand by their father's clothes and watch.

Soon the head is small and far away. The smell of bleach rises from the water. The waves no longer reach the shore.

CASSETTEPUNK

I got home in a sour mood. The journey had taken even longer than usual, with fifty minutes of unexplained gridlock near the City Hall, and the inevitable ideological confrontations had broken out among the trapped passengers. I was in my own world, footsore and brooding on work, and I only noticed the trouble when a group of twelve- or thirteen-year-olds began to mock me. They wore thin vests, pompadour hairstyles and no masks. They tried to grab my respirator and succeeded in tearing the membrane of my cape. After haranguing some other commuters and smearing wet kisses on the driver's Perspex screen, they forced open the doors and sauntered away through the motionless traffic.

When I turned into the cul-de-sac it was blocked with a vast heap of rubbish. Evidently a rogue bin lorry had chosen the front of our building to dump its load. The split bags and spills of rotting waste were alive with rats and pigeons. I stumbled through, gagging on the smell despite the respirator.

In trying to take off the cape, I damaged it beyond repair. I cursed and struggled free of the remnants in the hallway. Tapping on Ava's door got me no response, so I put my head into her room. Of course, she was locked in one of her games, with no sign that she had moved in the fourteen hours since I had last seen her. I fought down the urge to rip the wires from their sockets and give her a lecture. Instead I tiptoed through the mess, lifted her from the floor, and laid her on the bed. Encased in the gear she was like a puppet,

143

her joints loose, her head clumsy and faceless. Shivers ran through her limbs. I arranged pillows for support and left her to it.

In the kitchen I eyed the washing up, poured myself a Powers, and thumbed through my phone. This was exactly the time not to do it, I told myself. My lower front teeth were tingling. Nevertheless, I made the call. It rang for a long time; then I heard a protracted clatter, and a middle-aged woman asked indistinctly what I wanted. I had to repeat myself several times before I got across that I was hoping to speak to W. My own voice echoed in my ear, fed back by some technical fault. The woman on the line advised me to have a care for the tone I was taking, then hung up. I finished my whiskey and threw the glass into the sink.

As I was picking the shards from among the dirty dishes, Ava came in. She reached past me, filled a mug with water, and drained it in one swallow. She refilled it and drained it again.

'Sorry,' I said. 'Earlier.'

She looked at me. I cleared my throat, drummed my fingers on the table, began to say something, stopped. She raised her eyebrows, exasperated.

I said:

'Maybe I could try it sometime.'

> • <

Later, when I tried to remember, it seemed I had been visiting a great city – a metropolis the likes of which I had never seen or imagined. I clung to my guardian's hand in the crowds and she soothed me when I grew overwhelmed by the spectacle. One afternoon she took me for a treat to a famous teahouse with sea-green chandeliers that glimmered in the darkness, stained-glass windows of tigers and archers, aromas of fresh coffee, liquorice and maple. A smiling woman in an emerald dress played gypsy violin and I was allowed to drop a coin into the case.

Another time we witnessed an atrocity. A gang of men, hulking, horned like bulls, lashed with whips at pedestrians, forcing them to kneel. They tore the children from their loved ones and fastened chains around their necks. A white-haired gentleman rose to protest and was hacked down. The men's hindquarters were furred and filthy, their arms and bellies slabs of flesh. They sneered at the grieving people and began to drag their captives away.

Telling me to stay where I was, my guardian strode forward. She exchanged nods with two other young women who had arrived on the scene at the same moment. Then she grasped the air and drew from it a rapier made of sunlight. One of the other women was running upwards into space, mounting an invisible staircase, while the third sketched a symbol with her fingertips and became a panther. The three of them performed a brief dance at the end of which the captives were free and the miscreants lay weltering on the pavement.

My guardian took my hand, but I looked back to see the horned men dissolve. Their substance came apart and trailed into the sky like paper streamers.

> • <

Ava did not know that when I was small my father and I had played games. In those earliest days the software came on cassette tapes and was extremely slow and unreliable: we would spend twenty minutes listening to the cacophony of pips and jitters that meant a game was trying to load, but then the machine would hang and there would be nothing for it but to rewind the tape and try again. When we did get something working, he and I would lean together over the rubber keyboard, wholly absorbed by the simple electronic sounds and the small pulsing blocks of cyan, magenta and green on the monitor.

Later, for reasons I never grasped, he grew shy about it. The technology evolved – eight bits became sixteen, then thirty-two and sixty-four – but these exponential possibilities, it seemed, were something he had to refuse. Occasionally I tried to coax him back into playing with me, but each time the air curdled with his embarrassment and I knew I should not have brought it up.

I described all this to W, once, but I failed to convey its importance. I never mentioned it to Ava for fear that I would fail again. The games we played when I was small were so crude that she, Ava, would not have recognised them as games at all, but those memories never left me. Nothing since has filled me with such a longing for the future.

This time I was in the city for over a year. There was no way of leaving after the horned men staged their coup and installed their bull-headed leader as despot. Lacking identity papers, I lived on the streets for a time, begging and thieving, evading the police, the gas attacks and the wild children. I spied from the shadows on the rallies and triumphs, the punishment exhibitions and fiestas of forced marriage. Smoke poured from the nostrils of the great brass bulls and every alleyway stank of burnt meat. At length I was arrested for vagrancy and consigned to a work camp. Spending my days breaking rocks on demolition sites, I ceased to be sure that I had ever lived anywhere else.

Then, one night, a cloaked figure appeared in the darkness of the dormitory shed. She pressed her hand over my mouth and told me that a long journey lay before us. One camp guard almost raised the alarm, but my rescuer silenced him with a dagger like a crescent moon.

> • <

I drank and drank but the thirst did not let up all day. Ava would not speak to me. I could not understand why she was so upset, even if I had let my enthusiasm get the better of me a little. All I had wanted was to play, to share in her game. I would never be a native, nor even a settled citizen, I had said to myself, but surely I could become a competent visitor, well enough versed in manners and customs that she would not be ashamed to acknowledge me there. I could at least make a start; so, in the morning, when I knew she would be asleep, I had picked up the second headset.

When I next opened my eyes the gear was peeling away from my face and Ava was furious. Her own headset hung open around her neck. She had been forced to come in and get me, she said. Did I have any idea what that meant? Did I even begin to understand the consequences? What had I been trying to do?

Since then Ava had been at the kitchen table with her gear spread out in a tangle of wires and peripherals. She had fitted a holographic loupe to her eye and her fingers fluttered through invisible grids. She seemed to be racing against time.

I ran the tap into the sink, filled a glass with water and drank it. The stench of the rubbish tip filled the flat, though every window was shut. My eyeballs throbbed and a thin, hard ache was forcing its way through my skull. I had worn the headset for just under twenty-four hours.

At last Ava swore and dropped the loupe onto the table.

Look, I said, we can try again later, can't we? You can show me where I'm going wrong.

She stared at me.

You don't get it, do you? You actually have no idea.

She rubbed her face, then screwed the loupe into her eye and went back to work.

Please, she said, not looking up. Leave me alone.

The community was three hours away by coach. The fogged window showed me eroded fields studded here and there with derelict structures. Once they might have been refineries or power stations, but they no longer served a purpose.

Steady drizzle was falling when I trudged into the yard of what had once been a large farmhouse. Three women in overalls and work gloves came out of a side door. Two strode towards me while the third hung back, speaking into her phone. I waved. I had walked forty-five minutes from the coach stop, and what I wanted most was a sit down and a cup of tea. But the first of the women – tall and weathered, with thick salt-and-pepper hair tied up in a red cotton scarf – spread her hands as if to shepherd me back the way I had come.

No, I said, I'm not expected, I don't have an appointment. I was just passing.

I named W.

Just a check-in, really, I said. Our daughter. Not a problem.

I unfastened my respirator; no one here was wearing one. The women watched me. Several others had appeared in the yard now, dressed for physical work, carrying pickaxes and spades.

There is a process for requesting contact with a member of this community, said the tall woman.

Yes, I said, it's not like that. I just want to speak to her for a minute.

The tall woman spoke gently, almost fondly.

We are not obliged to give you what you want.

The woman on the phone ended her call and murmured something to the woman beside her, who nodded. Two more women walked from behind the house. One of them was W. When she noticed me, I gave her a little wave. Her companion laid a hand on her forearm and led her inside.

These tactics will not help you, said the tall woman. Do you understand that?

It was dark by the time I got on the coach back to the city.

> • <

Ava was lying on her bed in the foetal position, twitching and shivering, her head the bulky head of a puppet. Cables and peripherals were strewn across the floor. I had no way of telling how long she had been inside her game, if that was the right word for it. Perhaps she was in difficulties; perhaps they were doing something to her even now. I ought to grab the second headset and dive in, I told myself, to the rescue. That would make sense of things. Or I should tear the wires from their sockets and prise the gear from her face.

Instead I knelt by the bed, not quite daring to touch her. As the hours passed I grew concerned about dehydration. I brought in a jug of water and a cloth, with some idea that I might ease open the chin-piece enough to wet her lips. But I only waited. I drifted off to sleep, then woke in foolish terror to find her still curled on the bed.

Around dawn a blade of light glowed in the gap between the curtains. An hour later she stirred, then sat up, not surprised to find me watching. She helped me to my feet and told me to come with her. We had a long way to go.

She rose, and the headset and the rest of the gear fell from her as easily as dew, weightless, evaporating. As we stepped outside it seemed that she had not been wearing them at all.

THE OTHER SIDE OF THE
SHADOWS

The young man paces the office and makes wild gestures at the detective, who sits with his arms folded and his feet on the desk. The desk contains a loaded revolver and an empty bottle. The detective makes no apology for embracing the symbols of his profession, its trappings and tropes. His office is above a laundromat in a run-down part of the city. A trench coat hangs by the door. In matters of this kind he is a thorough romantic. He loves to see his name stencilled on the frosted glass. He loves to see his client's desperation. The romantic who loves what is seedy, broken and dangerous is the most sentimental romantic of all.

The young man has given his name as Otto Soroboru. He is a skinny, snake-hipped type with black hair cut in the asymmetric fringe that is *de rigueur* among privileged young males at present. Shoes cheap slip-on plimsolls, jeans up-to-the-minute, T-shirt a one-off made for him by a friend, leather jacket worth more than the detective makes in a month. Plays bass in an art band, deals narcotics within his social circle, lives off a trust fund. The kind of customer the detective reads in a blink.

'Sit down.'

The young man stops pacing but remains standing. The detective takes his feet off the desk. He loves to see the young man's desperation because this is the energy that he will take for himself when he takes the case. It will send him down the dark channels of the city, single-willed and relentless.

'How long has she been missing?'

'She's my twin sister,' Otto says. 'We've never been apart.'

'How long?'

Otto makes a hopeless gesture.

'Three nights. Some hours.'

The muscles of the detective's face do not move. At a juncture like this he'll offer a little of the PI swagger: stone cold, rock hard. It's what a client needs.

'Sit down,' he says. 'I charge three hundred a day, plus expenses.'

Otto sags into the chair.

'Thank you,' he says. 'Thank you.'

He passes over a photograph. A candid shot: she is outdoors, in sunshine, leaning on a railing, laughing, looking up, noticing the photographer exactly as the picture is taken. Her colouring matches her brother's, the thick black hair and the vodka-blue eyes. She has his thin frame and high cheekbones, but she also has a self-possession that he lacks. Her laughter looks intelligent, ironic. Her hair is loosely pinned up in a style that belongs to herself, not to fashion.

The detective pockets the photo.

'So talk to me,' he says.

Otto does not seem to understand.

'You've noticed something,' the detective says. 'Recently. Something strange about your sister.'

At this Otto lifts his chin and flares his nostrils.

'Nothing about Anna could be strange to me.'

The detective allows himself a smile: tight, mirthless, two seconds in duration.

'Reasons for her to go underground,' he says. 'If she's missing, odds are she wants to be. I'm looking for changes in routine, changes in behaviour. New friends or acquaintances.'

Otto shakes his head.

'Interests, places.'

This chimes somewhere. Otto's pupils shrink. He flicks the hair off his forehead.

'There was a place,' he says. 'She went a few times. I didn't like it. I asked her to stop.'

The detective's face does not move, but he feels the world tighten. He senses the dark channels of the city, out there, waiting.

'Talk to me.'

> • <

Working the Soroboru case, the detective walks down a street. Broken panes, boarded fronts, litter blowing free. He passes into the wedge of shadow that lies under a railway bridge. Tropes and trappings. More essential than the trench coat, the revolver or the hard-bitten demeanour is the shadow. Shadows lie everywhere in the city. The detective's role is to walk through them and come out on the other side.

He turns down an access lane between the blind backs of warehouses. A flight of steps descends to a door at basement level. There is no sign or marker, no evidence that the building is in use. He tries the door, then takes out a roll of locksmith's tools.

Pathos of the nightclub by day. Decor heavy on the old gilt, dull mirrors and dusty velvet. Nostalgia for a more innocent decadence. The detective circles the room, checking the booths, squatting to touch a mark on the floor, pausing at the bar. Red wine dark in green bottles, white wine yellow in clear bottles.

One of the velvet curtains conceals another door.

The room beyond is set up for a cabaret, with small circular tables ranged across the floor and a low stage at one end. The walls are plastered with old posters for vaudeville shows and travelling circuses. On the stage stands a curious object. It seems to be an item of furniture, but what manner of furniture, made for what function, the detective cannot tell. It resembles a chair – or two chairs, spindly and elaborate, that have been built around and through one another. The parts interrupt one another so that it would be impossible to actually sit down on the thing. It could be a piece of sculpture, intentionally useless, but that explanation does not do much for the detective.

He takes out his camera, snaps, blinks away the after-flash. The object is worn and battered, as if it has been in use for some time. He steps up on the stage and takes a couple more photographs. Each pop of the flash throws the room into a new tableau, dropping stark shadows on the floor.

The last flash reveals a figure standing in the doorway, tall and bulky, draped in a long, loose coat. In the purple blindness that follows, the figure flees and the detective chases, knocking over tables and chairs as they blunder through the nightclub.

The detective trips into the street, dazzled. He can hear footsteps retreating but the figure is already out of sight. Fast for a big guy. The footsteps clattering off the warehouse backs have an irregular rhythm, quick and complex, as if he is doing a tap-dance as he runs. The detective sprints to the corner, but he knows when a quarry has got clear. He turns back, walks along the street.

> • <

How many mini-marts like this one exist in the city? Small, nameless, run-down, struggling. Shabby with an intrinsic shabbiness. In the detective's view, a shop like this survives because it is so outmoded, so hopelessly local. Clinging to a single site in space and time, it is beneath the notice of the chains and franchises which enjoy a more abstract form of existence, present everywhere at once, mapping themselves into the city's future forever.

Watched by the cashier, the detective walks along the aisles and passes through a bead curtain at the back of the shop. He continues through a stockroom and into a poorly lit corridor, which he follows until he comes up against a man sitting on a stool in front of a door.

The man gets to his feet. Tough. Two heads taller than the detective and bulky. Nose flattened, ears smashed out of shape, male pattern baldness shaved to stubble. Biceps the same size as his head. Overall a classic look. You could put him in a leopard skin and a handlebar moustache. The detective knows the tough from previous encounters, and the tough knows the detective. They acknowledge this by offering one another no signs of recognition whatsoever.

The detective gazes at the black T-shirt stretched taut across the slabs of the man's chest. Then he looks up, catches the tough's eye.

'Do we have to do this?'

The tough smiles.

>•<

Alan Raven, holding the tip of his tongue between his teeth, uses a fine brush to paint an arcane symbol on the skull of a rat. Raven is seated at the worktable in the centre of his study, where two lamps make a bright pool in the gloom. His face is obscured by the small circular spectacles, the long lank hair, the beard that forks into two thick points.

Raven looks up as the door is smashed open by the falling body of his tough. The detective steps across, rubbing his knuckles. The tough may be twice his size, but the detective knows his business. He knows the tough has an old injury in the left knee. He knows how to take advantage of that, and he knows how to follow up a surgical kick with a sucker punch.

Raven lays down his brush and blows gently on the rat skull to dry the ink. Then he reaches for his pestle and mortar and grinds the skull into dust. The detective watches. Raven's study has its touches of gangster ostentation. One of his safes stands open, showing the stacks of cash and the clear plastic bags of powder inside. A chrome-plated Beretta lies at one end of the worktable. At the same time, other interests are in evidence, in the shelves of esoteric volumes that line the walls, the divinatory equipment, the pallid objects in jars, the hermetic charts. The detective can appreciate Raven's sense of himself. It's a mash-up but it works.

'You owe me a favour.'

Raven tips the bone-dust into a clear plastic bag and seals it. Then he steeples his fingers. His spectacles gleam and he grins, showing two long front teeth.

The detective hands him the camera. Raven thumbs through the photographs and hands it back. He is no longer smiling.

'You're investigating a disappearance,' he says.

'Maybe.'

'Delete those pictures,' Raven says. 'Pay back your fee, take a fortnight's holiday, and don't ever mention this again.'

'A woman is missing,' says the detective.

Raven picks up one of his tarot decks, shuffles it and puts it down. He peers over the top of his spectacles.

'Forget it.'

The detective does not move. Raven sighs and leans back in his chair.

'Plato tells us that in the beginning, human beings were double,' he says. 'Four hands and four feet, one head with two faces. Four eyes, four ears, two mouths and two privy members. At that time, Plato tells us, we were complete and we suffered no desire. But then, for our sins, the gods split us in two, and ever since we have been half-creatures, forever searching for the other one that completes us. Of course, you're familiar with the myth. No?'

'Raven,' says the detective. 'Talk to me.'

'It's a pretty story, isn't it? As a story, I mean. Nothing you'd want to take too seriously, I'd say. But certain people would disagree.'

Raven gets up to search his shelves, then lays a book in the pool of light. A curiously proportioned volume, the shape and size of a brick, bound in greasy leather, age-blackened.

'Certain people can't let stories lie,' he says. 'And when a story like that becomes more than just a story, it's not so pretty any more.'

Raven pushes the book towards the detective. He has opened it at an illustration: a dense, intricate woodcut, its tobacco-brown lines stamped deep into the vellum, embellished with pink and green dyes. The detective realises what he is looking at. The woodcut shows an item of furniture identical to the one he photographed in the nightclub.

'This particular volume is only six hundred years old,' Raven says. 'The tradition goes back much further, of course.'

In the woodcut the entangled chairs are occupied. Sitting in the double chair is a monster: a hideous fusion of two human beings, their anatomies altered and agglutinated so that the thing precisely fits its bizarre throne. Eight disarticulated limbs. Two torsos melded into an asymmetrical and elongated trunk, all threaded through the slots and gaps of the chair. Two necks twine to a single heart-shaped head, on which two faces wear expressions of saintly ecstasy.

'I don't understand,' the detective says.

'It can be done,' says Raven. 'Anything can be done by those with the will. Today, in this very city, there are those who are determined to regain the unity that was stolen by the jealous gods.'

The detective gazes at the woodcut.

'A cult.'

'Call it what you like.'

The detective can feel the walls drawing close on either side. What is between him and Raven is a kind of voltage. The corrupt complacency of the magician is what the detective needs now, because he needs this anger that will propel him into the shadows, into the dark channels where he is to go.

'What would they want with a young woman?'

'I can tell you that,' Raven says. 'I can even tell you where to find them. But you won't thank me if I do.'

'What do they want with her?'

Raven takes off his spectacles and rubs his eyes.

'It's not easy,' he says. 'The procedure is – costly. Less than pleasant.'

Raven purses his pale lips, and appears to choose his words carefully.

'In practice, uniting two human beings requires the – ah – the contribution of a third.'

This is the point where the detective might break something. Pick up the astral globe on Raven's side-table and put it through the little painted-over window in the back wall. Anything to get some light in here and some clean air. Raven, who now seems to find the situation amusing, is shuffling his tarot again. He deals three cards. The Lovers. The Tower. The Fool. The detective does not have time for this. But he does not break anything: he only puts his fists on the table.

'Talk,' he says. 'You're telling me they want her for what? A ritual? Sacrifice?'

Raven shuffles his cards back into the pack. He points at the woodcut in the ancient book.

'Look more closely.'

Following Raven's ragged fingernail, the detective notices a new detail in the illustration. He thought the monster was a ghastly combination of two people, but this is not exactly so. The heart-shaped head bears two ecstatic faces, yes, but now the detective can see a third face. It is almost unrecognisable as human, melting into the asymmetric torso, but the printmaker, dead these six centuries, has worked an expression of still-living agony into the distorted features. From this face a network of veins and sinews runs across the whole anatomy. The third individual has been reduced to a web of flesh holding the other two together.

Raven shows his teeth, pleased the detective grasps the point, pleased at his squeamishness.

'I'm telling you,' he says, closing the book and caressing its greasy cover, 'that they need connective tissue.'

> • <

Some parts of the city are unknown even to the detective. This is a simple function of the city's size – its sprawl, its density, its depth. No single lifetime, however dedicated, would be enough to learn the city completely, and the wise are those who understand that their knowledge will always be unfinished. The detective knows this. He knows that his knowledge is always inexorably shrinking, because the city's condition is flux and the realities that emerge from its ever-rolling boil outpace all that the detective, or anyone else, can discover.

The detective walks through streets he has never seen before. Old posters flap loose on a hoarding, flashing a repeating design of clowns and acrobats in red, green and yellow. He walks through neighbourhoods in deepening stages of neglect. Figures watch him from doorways and corners. Now some young men drift almost casually across the pavement to block his way, but the detective makes certain adjustments to his bearing and the men disperse before he reaches them. Now the detective cuts through a lattice of alleyways and into a deserted avenue.

Dilapidated frontages rise behind yards overgrown to thickets. Dust blinds panes of high windows. Here the day is ending. A footfall echoes. The detective walks a little further, scanning the buildings. The street waits. He retraces his steps, reaches into a doorway, pulls someone out of it and slams him against the wall.

Otto Soroboru. His heels graze pavement. The detective has two fistfuls of expensive leather.

'You don't follow me.'

'I can't just sit and wait,' Otto says. 'I need to find her.'

The detective lets go.

'You don't want to be here.'

Otto tugs his jacket straight. A great bloody seal has broken along the base of the sky and the stain is spreading up through the gaps between the houses.

'Where are we?' Otto asks.

The detective is looking at the last house on the street. The largest and the most dilapidated. It stands by itself, surrounded by a high brick wall that has fallen in several places.

'Here.'

> • <

They step around an iron gate hanging by one hinge. The house is a squat, baggy shape pitched in this open lot, its walls tinted by the sunset. Shadows reach through the long grass. French doors stand open with weeds knotted through the broken panes. The detective steps into a room that has ivy on the walls.

Elsewhere in the city, Alan Raven picks up a tarot deck.

The detective moves into the house with Otto a few steps behind. The rooms close around them. The windows are boarded. The beam of the detective's torch plays around the vault of a hallway. The floorboards are soft with rot.

The detective tips the torch-beam into a room where two wingback chairs face an empty fireplace. A funnel of wreckage hangs where the ceiling has collapsed.

The detective hears a noise. Footsteps above, tapping out a quick, irregular rhythm.

Raven shuffles his tarot.

The detective leads Otto across the hall. At the foot of the stairs, he pauses to draw his revolver. They climb one flight. On the landing they freeze. Footsteps behind the wall. The detective raises his torch and his weapon, wrists crossed. The light flashes the length of the corridor. They hear a second set of footsteps behind the other wall, with the same tap-dance rhythm. The detective twists on his heel, throwing the light down the corridor, but there is no one to be seen.

Raven begins to lay out the cards.

The detective and Otto climb another flight of stairs. They look into a room where an iron bedstead lies like a rusted-out cage. The boards are coming away from the windows and bars of bloody light show through. The detective leads on to the end of the corridor, where a stepladder hangs from a trapdoor in the ceiling.

Raven has laid out three cards in a row. The Anatomy. The Shipwreck. The Amphisbaena.

The detective and Otto climb into an attic room that must cover the whole footprint of the house. More than half the roof slates lie scattered on the floor among drifts of dead leaves. The rafters, broken down by weather, lean like leafless trees. The zenith is as dark and clear as green glass. The evening air is cool.

Anna Soroboru looks calm, healthy, well-rested, without trauma. She wears a simple cotton dress.

'Otto,' she says.

'I came as fast as I could.'

'And you brought someone with you.'

The twins turn towards the detective.

'I think he'll do,' says Otto.

'Oh, he'll do.'

The piece of furniture beside Anna is spindly and elaborate. Its parts interrupt one another in such a way that nothing recognisable as a human being could sit down in it. Compared with the object the detective saw in the nightclub, this is a superior example. Its lines curve like scalpels.

Raven turns a second row of cards. The Mirrors. The Leviathan. The Taint of the Fairground.

Several figures detach themselves from shadows in far parts of the room. Their features are invisible under their hoods. They are tall and bulky, dressed in long, loose coats. They move forward with a curious gait to encircle the detective and the twins.

Otto is fumbling in his jacket, clutching at his pockets.

'Looking for this?'

The detective shows a pistol. A Saturday-night special, cheap and flashy.

'Took care of it down in the street.'

He points the pistol at Otto's chest. At the same time, he levels his own snub-nosed revolver at Anna. The hooded figures keep their distance.

'Hands,' says the detective. 'So the way I see it, you kids are into some creepy mojo. What you get out of it I don't know and I don't want to.'

Anna and Otto are smiling at one another.

'Thing is,' the detective says, 'I know my business. And I don't appreciate getting picked for a sucker.'

'Yet here you are,' Anna says.

The detective's eyes dart around, measuring distances, counting players, anticipating moves. He has come to the centre of something. He has allowed himself to be led, as if he did not know what was happening. He has done this in order to make his argument: to show these degenerates that there are consequences. He has come here to break something, and he has a good idea of where to start.

He swings both the pistols to point at the chair-like object.

Otto shouts and dives forward, grabbing for the weapons. The detective flicks his wrist and the young man hits the floor. When he looks up he is bleeding from the bridge of his nose.

'Touchy,' says the detective.

'If you damage it,' Anna says, 'you won't leave this house.'

The detective is about to reply, but an instinct jabs. He ducks and spins as one of the hooded figures grabs from behind. Too close: he did not hear the goon sneaking up. He does not know how that happened, but there is no time to think about it now because the others are closing in. The detective knows his business. He raises his revolver and unloads two rounds into the chest of the nearest figure. The tidiest way to resolve the situation. Put that one down, give the others a reason to hesitate, put the detective in charge for the few seconds he needs.

But the figure has not gone down. It keeps coming. He gives it two more rounds, then empties the rest of the cylinder into another one of the figures. Neither seems to notice. The detective is puzzled. The hooded figures are larger than they should be. He thinks of wrestlers, lovers, two bodies grappled in a terrible closeness.

Blood soaks their garments but they are still coming. Everything is moving more slowly than it should. The hoods close in. Puzzled by his own sluggishness, he lifts Otto's cheap pistol and pulls the trigger until the clip is empty. It does not seem to make a difference.

Raven turns the cards. The Premature Burial. The Child. The Tree of the World.

'We've waited so long,' Otto says.

Anna smiles at her twin.

'Not much longer now.'

The weapons fall from the detective's hands. Anna and Otto only have eyes for one another. They are standing on either side of the chair that is not a chair.

'It can be done,' says Otto, as if reciting a rote phrase.

'By those with the will,' says Anna.

In the course of his work the detective has often been manhandled, but the toughs, heavies and hard-men of the city have never displayed such strength as he feels in the hands that now grasp his limbs. His feet leave the floor, and struggle is irrelevant as he is carried towards the brother and the sister.

Anna and Otto watch his approach. Otto's face is bloody, but their expressions are identical, serene, sympathetic.

'We're grateful,' says one.

'It means a lot,' says the other.

Raven contemplates the tarot he has cast, the nine arcana laid out three by three.

The twins are moving closer to one another, and between them stands the object that is like a chair but is not one. No human being could sit in it, but somehow it seems that they are able to sit. The effect is like an optical illusion. Their bodies distort as if hidden mirrors are built into the structure. As if an act of surgery, exquisite and total, is immanent in the object. Their bodies twist and elongate, disjoint and open. Within a few moments they are a spectacle beyond anything the detective wishes to understand. And yet their faces are as beautiful as ever, and their large, clear eyes rest on him with every sign of pleasant anticipation.

'Don't worry,' says one of them. 'You'll still be conscious.'

'Oh, completely conscious of everything.'

Raven, weary and a little disgusted with himself, sweeps up the cards and shuffles them into the pack.

The inhumanly strong hands are carrying the detective forward, and now the structure of the object reveals itself to him so that he glimpses his own place in the scheme. 'No,' he says, but there is no choice. The twins are in their change, changing ever more radically now as their third draws closer, and although they are no longer capable of ordinary speech the detective can understand them perfectly, and he has no choice but to hear their invitation and to heed it.

Come and join us, they are saying. Join us together.

THE WALKER

Where did I get the idea? All I know is that my suspicions began as soon as I arrived in the city. I had come here like everyone else, in search of the usual things: a room, a life, a district whose alleys and gardens I would call mine. I wanted to ride the trams, haunt the cafés and dine on the street food. I wanted to be changed beyond recognition. I was not asking for more than that, and I certainly did not intend to write any of this down. Even then I knew that to do so would be a mistake.

But good intentions are not enough, and one sunny evening I stood on the pavement transfixed by the sight of an ornamental tree beside a set of iron railings. It was nothing, just a fragment of the city, but standing there in the smell of exhaust and magnolia I found myself unable to make sense of it. I could not move on. Commuters were brushing past. Then a hand tugged at my sleeve and I turned to find a shabby figure looking up at me, grey-faced, half-starved but smiling as if he understood my predicament. He opened his mouth to speak.

Appalled, I fled, but the damage had been done. In the weeks that followed I fell out with my friends, caught a persistent cold and failed to keep my appointments. I grew weary and aggrieved. Running late for work, I saw that face in the crowd. The flesh was patterned with bruises as if it had undergone surgery. Everyone knows what you're after, I wanted to say as I pushed past: I have my own story to get on with. But did I still believe that? The idea was with me and I could not shake it.

Indications mounted. One night I dreamed that cities were built not from iron and brick but from memories, and when I woke up I was on the point of recalling where I had seen this place before. Later, browsing book stalls at the market, I opened an old paperback at the words *remember how you came to this city...* I left quickly, but not before I had noticed the grey figure watching at a distance. It trailed me through the streets as if to demand credit where it was due.

I am nervous, of course, but I will not be leaving the city. That would not help. The figure is always with me now, its hand always on my sleeve, and it is no longer willing to be ignored. Although I pretend otherwise I hear its voice all the time. We both know there is nothing I can do. In spite of myself, I have begun to listen.

THE HEIGHTS OF SLEEP

The novelist J.S. Gaunt gets described as a writer's writer, but for me he's more than that. I sometimes think he's the writer who made me what I am.

When I met him, fifteen years after I started reading his work, I told him so. This was one of the many ways I embarrassed myself during those ninety minutes of conversation in a Soho coffee shop. In person, Gaunt was gentle-mannered, accommodating, sometimes lost for words – the man was unlike the writing in all these respects – but even so, I spent the encounter disoriented, saying foolish things. Some books come to feel as if they belong to you alone. And then you find yourself face to face with the person who made them, and what are you supposed to do?

I was seventeen years old when I discovered Gaunt. I knew I was going to study English Lit at university – in those days a reasonably modest ambition – but alongside my curricular reading I had a taste for the more disreputable stuff. I thought I had a radical streak because I liked horror and space opera and dungeonpunk fantasy in just the same way I liked Austen, Dickens and Woolf. I was a rebel in my own head because I refused to make a distinction.

I kept coming across Gaunt's name in magazine interviews with genre writers I admired. When asked about their influences, they all said the same thing: J.S. Gaunt was a stylist and a visionary, and it was a crime his work was not more widely known. I needed no further encouragement to make a day trip to Charing Cross Road. Tucked away on the top floor in Foyles, I found a copy of the old omnibus edition of the Masquador novels, with its ugly cover and its selection of cryptic critical praise on the back. '*Perturbing fables, twisted and occasionally perverse*'; '*The Man Who Was Thursday as rewritten by Ballard*'; '*The Alexandria Quartet meets Lovecraft via Djuna Barnes*'; '*These hallucinations would crumble if they were not sustained by prose of such unfaltering precision*'; '*From its pulp-fiction roots the Masquador cycle blooms as a strange new flower of evil*'.

It was an ideal introduction to Gaunt. I tore through the three novels. In *The Silver Curtain* the story of supernatural intrigue was stylish but largely conventional, but *A Conspiracy of Wasps* twisted the same scenario into baffling surrealism. And then came *Among the Masquadors*: I had never finished a book with such a strong intuition that it contained a hidden pattern, some secret I needed to understand. The omnibus concluded with the handful of short stories usually known as *The Masquador Dances*: really they were no more than sketches for the mythos, but I combed each of them for clues to what it all meant.

While I was a student I read all the Gaunt I could find. I tracked down his first two novels, *The Remnants* and *The Foal*, in the library stacks. They were set in 1970s Manchester, and dealt with the adventures of bohemian young men who were mystified by women and angry with the world. There was a lot of cynical sex and hippie philosophy, broken up by moments of unexplained violence, betrayal and magic. They were not great, but I read them studiously. There was a thrill in recognising Gaunt's way with a sentence, his daredevil adverbs and ruthless commas, highly characteristic and already there in his earliest stuff. From the beginning he was using some of his favourite motifs: iridescent green beetles, bereaved women, poker, strange buried machinery, one-eyed cats, a pair of clasped hands suddenly taking on the appearance of a face. These images, and certain key phrases relating to them, recurred through all the Gaunt I had read, as if they were a tarot that he dealt and re-dealt, finding new meanings each time.

I read the books he had published in the twenty-odd years since the Masquador sequence. It took me a long time to get through *The Ablation Colony*, *The Heart's Retreat* and *Crocodile Fires*, though all three of those novels are so short. For a while I was defeated by their density and their refusal to belong to any obvious category, and even when I had finished them I had an odd feeling I should not move on. It was as if I had glimpsed something lurking in the edges of the fictions, as if getting the three books into alignment would reveal a figure that had nothing to do with what the stories seemed to be about.

When I tried introducing friends to Gaunt, I always ended up regretting it, always feeling they had not quite seen what I was getting at. It gives me the same shiver that I get when I remember stupid things I did at that age: blurting out private matters to people I had just met, getting infatuated with girls I did not like, making obnoxious remarks because I did not know what I believed. That urge to share Gaunt's work was no different.

Once I ran into another fan. I was in the union canteen, reading my new hardback of his novel *Form*, and she came over. We enthused for a while over the sheer fact that he had written another; I told her I was only up to page seventy-nine but so far it was astonishing, that you could see how it grew out of what he had been doing in short stories like 'Caffè Atrocità' and 'Dancing the Disaster', but it went so much further. She begged me not to say more because she was going to read it the first chance she got. It flashed across my mind that maybe we would start a relationship, an affair. Maybe this was how it was done – we'd be thrown into it by shared passionate intimacy with Gaunt's work. Instead we found we had nothing else to say.

Form was the longest book Gaunt had written. The reviews said it was his most ambitious but also his most accessible. I was not sure about that, but it was a major feat, big and picaresque, with its five protagonists on their entangled odysseys through the past, the present, the future and several parallel universes. The satirical edge was sharper than ever, and the ending was as bleak and enigmatic as anything he had written. Obviously it was going to be understood as a comedy of despair at contemporary culture, and its inventive vigour would be seen as redeeming its nihilism. But as I read, I found myself dwelling on smaller details. When Lulu Zhong finds her daughter, why is the nail bar where they meet called 'Rainbow Foam' – the same name Gaunt gave to a bioengineered psychedelic virus in a story he published in a New Wave magazine more than thirty years earlier? Why is Rossi quite so frightened when he mistakes Lamb's face for his own in the mirror? What's with all the molecular chemistry stuff? Why does Dorian Scurf, who first appeared as the proprietor of the junk shop in *The Silver Curtain* and turned up again in *The Heart's Retreat* to usher the protagonist to his doom, now feature as an occult card sharp? And what's actually at stake in the last game? I had dozens of questions along these lines.

A year or so after *Form* was published, I had an argument with a young woman. I was about to travel two hundred miles by National Express to a provincial book festival where Gaunt was making an appearance, and the young woman, to whom I would later get married, ribbed me for being so into a writer no one else had heard of. I responded so humourlessly that I still cringe to think of it, getting indignant and asking if she had even read him. She said she had tried one of his books but found its attitude so singularly male that she lost interest. I fumed for the whole coach journey and decided she and I had no future. As for the author talk, I did not remember much of it afterwards. Gaunt was a slight, trim man in jeans and a hooded top, who kept his feet flat on the floor and had a way of pressing his palms together between his knees. The slate-grey hair was cropped close to the small, handsome head, and the steel-rimmed spectacles flashed when they caught the lights. At one point the chair quoted Henry James: 'We work in the dark – we do what we can – we give what we have,' and so on. I thought Gaunt was going to skewer the man's pomposity, but instead he said that for him writing was like sleep. It takes you to the same place you go when you fall asleep, he said, but the gravity is reversed. Up becomes down, so you can't get there by falling. You have to climb. When the chair invited questions from the audience I did not raise my hand.

> • <

Gaunt followed *Form* with a novel called *Harm*, ostensibly a sequel although it bore little resemblance. It was a quarter of the length, and instead of a rambling epic it was a tight three-hand psychodrama set in a single location. *Harm*'s nameless characters do not appear in *Form*, but the sharp-eyed reader recognises that the isolated, decaying manse where the woman, the man and the daughter play out their catastrophe is the same house where the Nyberg children go missing in the earlier book. I reviewed *Harm* for the *Times Literary Supplement*. I had got into book-reviewing the year I graduated, when I sent the *TLS* a clipping of something I had written in a student paper and they sent me back a copy of some novel and a deadline for six hundred words. Since then I had been doing a piece every few months, and had not ceased to be amazed at what a painful process it was to review a book. Less harrowing than my attempts at fiction, for sure, but its own special kind of misery. In a review there are so many ways to be lazy, dishonest, timid, ignorant, bullying, spurious, inexact, ungenerous or unjust, and so few ways to be true. Reviewing Gaunt was ten times worse than usual. I re-read everything he had published, then spent most of a week on my opening paragraph, trying to encapsulate his career, his style, his preoccupations and his significance to date in eighty words. I scribbled all over my review copy. I wrote nine different plot summaries and rejected them all as too reductive. I realised the apparently straightforward action of the book was in fact irreducibly ambiguous. I kept leafing through Gaunt's collected short fiction and finding clues in stories he had written over four decades. Stories like 'Little Quadratics', 'Spider Dimension', 'Singularity Blues', 'Disco Lazarus': all bore vitally on this new phase of work, and what was more, the post-apocalypse sections of *Crocodile Fires* now had to be seen in a completely different light. I could not imagine how it was possible for a life's writing all to map together like a great fractal falling into itself forever on every scale at once. What it was or what it meant, what figure might show itself at last, I had no idea.

A couple of months later I went along to the *TLS* summer party, out of some impulse to drink warm white wine with several hundred people who would all prefer to be at home. To my surprise, Gaunt was there among the moleskin jackets and balding heads. He sometimes wrote for the paper, but he did not seem the sort to come to drinks parties. He was in motorcycle leathers, not holding a drink, listening closely to a woman in a purple shawl. I felt I should speak to him – perhaps I would always regret it if I did not – but I couldn't think of a single thing to say. I hovered for a while and then, murmuring, 'Hey, I'm no one you know but I've read all your books and what do you think about that,' I left.

> • <

I wrote a book of my own. I thought publishing a novel would answer some question I had not fully articulated. I was not so naive as to imagine life would change in any practical way, but I had a notion that when I saw the thing in print I would know why it had been worth doing: why I had spent four years of evenings and weekends shut in my room, instead of giving that time to the young woman who found Gaunt's work excessively male, and to our daughter. I expected that, once published, the book would feel different from all the failed fragments, terrible stories and unworkable novels I had been writing and discarding for as long as I could remember. But when I picked up the first proof copy I found that each page was a mass of flaws and vulnerabilities. The book's whole purpose, it appeared, was to expose the limitations of its author. The debt to Gaunt was painfully obvious. I had known he was one of my touchstones, but now I saw I had produced nothing but a thin imitation. Even my title seemed shamefully Gauntian, and for a while I cast around for an alternative that would at least throw readers off the scent. But nothing else fit, and I had to accept that the book was called *The Heights of Sleep*.

I had slept poorly in the last weeks of the final draft, lying half-awake for hours with structural problems flailing in my head. Then I would slip into a dream in which the world was a single infinite house in whose grey rooms and gardens I kept accosting family and strangers, trying to convince them of a peril that had been revealed to me alone. Every time I dreamt it there was the same shock as I grasped that they knew the abominable truth already: they had been living with it all along. I had never had a recurring dream before, and I grew concerned it might not go away. But once the book was signed off I stopped remembering my dreams.

My editor asked for a list of writers to send advance reading copies, the idea being that if they liked the book they might give us a quote for promotional purposes. I hesitated before including Gaunt's name. He would see at once that I had written a knock-off of his early stuff; he'd be furious, or he'd pity me, or sue me for plagiarism. In the end, though, I decided to send him a copy. If not now, I told myself, then when? He probably wouldn't read it anyway. And in the days that followed I felt lightened, as if I had been freed from a compulsion.

A few weeks later my editor forwarded me a message from J.S. Gaunt. He was grateful for the copy of *The Heights of Sleep*. He never gave publicity endorsements, but he had enjoyed the book. He looked forward to my next one, and in the meantime I should get in touch if I ever wanted to meet up.

> • <

A bright, cramped Italian coffee bar: grubby Formica, Soho crowding past the window, light echoing off steel surfaces, the espresso machine's snarl. I got there early and was immediately mired in logistics. Which table? Should I order now? Would I recognise him? How should I make myself known? I was rearranging my coat on the back of my seat when I saw him standing in the entrance, blinking as if the scene were a surprise. Close-cropped hair no longer grey but white. Leather jacket, hoodie, worn jeans, biker boots, messenger bag. My pulse beat in my temples as I stood up. I wanted this to be over already, and at the same time I wanted us to hit it off so well that before we knew it we'd be falling out of a late bar in the small hours of tomorrow morning.

He ordered a double espresso, and I asked for the same. My copy of *Form*, which I was planning to ask him to sign, lay on the table between us. He did and did not look as I had expected. He looked like a man of his age, with liver-spots at his hairline, grey hairs in his nostrils and a trace of milk in his pale blue eyes. I had taken up poker as a result of reading his accounts of the game. He saw it as a practice in which you could discover your illusions about the world: not as a metaphor for anything, but poker as a way of actually confronting yourself. I wanted to tell him how this idea had beguiled me, but it seemed a weird thing to bring up, and besides, I was hardly in a position to swap poker stories with a veteran of the card table. I had played a few nights with friends and then let it slide.

I emptied two sachets of sugar into my coffee. Gaunt sipped his straight. I told him that one of my most vivid memories was of lying in a park in hot July sun, smelling the chlorine from an outdoor pool and reading the whole of *Among the Masquadors* in an afternoon. I told him I was extremely interested in the way he had taken his stories 'Taboo Parade' and 'The Insufferablist' and crossbred them to produce his novella *Persephone Potts*. I told him I was all too conscious that my review of *Harm* hadn't even scratched the surface of what was really going on in that book. I told him I had a theory that whatever the daughter sees in the upstairs bathroom is linked with the crooked murder investigation in the central section of *Form*. I told him I had read on the internet that he had finished the third book in the sequence, and I couldn't wait to see how the pattern was going to unfold. He asked me what I was working on now.

I was dumbfounded less by the question than by the fact I had not thought to have an answer ready. I stumbled through a couple of half-formed ideas. Then, confused, I told him how nervous I had been about sending him *The Heights of Sleep*, given the book's debt to his work.

Gaunt looked puzzled.

'I hadn't noticed a resemblance,' he said.

At that, we both seemed to lose the thread of the conversation. Gaunt looked at the ceiling and I swallowed the sludge at the bottom of my cup.

He began to talk about Cynthia Cleaver. She had been kind to him when he was starting out, he said. There had been one night, around the time of his second book, when she had asked him round for dinner. I leaned forward, excited, because – it now seemed obvious – this must be the reason distinguished writers met with tyros: to pass on this kind of story.

Cynthia Cleaver was an important name to me, not that this was unusual on my part. She was the kind of writer I could only have admired more if she had been a little less well-known. I had first come to her when I studied *The Fox's Tower* as an A-level text, but it took me years to realise what a figure she actually was. Cynthia Cleaver: prolific experimental novelist in genres from kitchen-sink gothic to surreal satirical SF to postmodernist Victorian pastiche, leftist campaigner, feminist provocateur, folklorist, writer of stage plays, screenplays and radio plays, translator of *Beowulf* and the *Arabian Nights*, travel writer, pioneer of long-form first-person cultural criticism, tireless polemicist, reviewer of everything from literary fiction to sixties fashion to punk rock to pornography to political rallies. She had died in middle age, eleven years after I was born. I had a shelf of her books.

Gaunt was explaining that in the late seventies Cleaver liked to invite young writers for dinner, two or three at a time, at her house beside Hampstead Heath. She would roast a joint and serve it in her little basement kitchen, then pour the wine and hold court. Along with Gaunt, Cleaver had served dinner that night to Will Stagg and Charlotte Borden, both of whom at that time were trendy youngsters who had done a few things. Stagg was as much of a dick then as now, Gaunt said, and Borden was going through a troubled period. As for the young Gaunt himself, he was callow, arrogant and rude. He was convinced they were laughing up their sleeves at him and that they thought he should be mopping floors for a living. He shook his head.

'I must have talked some rubbish that night.'

But Cleaver, he said, had been equal to his shortcomings as a dinner guest. Briskly, discreetly, with a glint of irony – and doing the same for the other two idiots at the table – she had coaxed him into loosening his grip on his own ego. She conducted an acerbic conversation, demanding hard thought and quick wits from her guests. She did not let you off on any particular point, but she drew you up to her level. The atmosphere in Cynthia Cleaver's kitchen told you that writing was too serious a matter for writers to be allowed to get in its way.

'I saw things differently after that,' Gaunt said.

We ordered more coffees. Out of sheer discomfiture, I picked up the copy of *Form* and opened it at random. It was the passage where Vincent gets kidnapped. I told Gaunt – chuckling at how unlikely it sounded now I came to say it out loud – that I had always had this notion of something hidden in his work, something with its own separate existence. He looked blank. I began to speak faster and less coherently as I tried to get across what I meant. Not a point or an idea, I said, not a pattern or a design, but something big, something else, something you've been getting at all this time. A kind of fractal shape, so we have to know how to calculate it before it can appear. I wasn't explaining well, I said. I heard a pleading note in my voice. In that moment I felt that I was not asking Gaunt to confirm the existence of the secret figure, but to deny it.

He did not reply. He was not surprised by what I had said, only embarrassed by the jumbled emotional demand I seemed all of a sudden to be making. Twenty minutes later we parted at a bus stop.

> › • ‹

That day, seven years ago, was the last time I saw Gaunt. Life has changed since then, but I've been working on my next book the whole time. I still have a way to go. It's an ambitious one, I suppose.

Encouragement is important, and I often look at my copy of Gaunt's novel *Germ*, which arrived in the post a month after we met in the coffee shop. It has an inscription from the author. The date, my name, his name, and one other word: *Upward*. When I first saw that, the meaning was clear. Now it seems less so. I emailed Gaunt to thank him for the book, but there was no reply.

For a long time I blamed myself for not having struck up a friendship. Now and then I felt I had defeated the whole purpose of writing *The Heights of Sleep*. The regret was useful, though, because it drove me on in the early stages of this new book. I liked to imagine that when it was finished, it would redeem that failure. It would show beyond a doubt that I understood.

Gaunt dropped out of sight after *Germ* was published. He was not reviewing. Nothing fresh came up when I searched for his name. My editor, in one of the conversations we still occasionally had, told me she had heard he was working on a new project. I imagined him in a late surge, setting out on a new inward journey at an age when most would be content to rest on an honourable career. Then one day I saw an arts and culture item which said the cult author J.S. Gaunt had died at the age of seventy-six after a short illness.

I could hardly claim to have known the man, but it did have an impact. We would never have another book. We would never have another inimitably Gauntian sentence. For a while I stopped writing, the first shock turning into gloomy months in which I could not see the point. The woman with whom I had once argued over a literary festival was sympathetic, but I knew she thought it would not be such a bad thing if this was the end of my attempt at a second book. It might be good news for us all. It was a pity she felt like that, and a pity I did not try harder to change her mind.

But setting a project aside can produce new insights, and soon I was seeing things I had not noticed before. Unfinished as it was, the work in progress showed traces of a pattern or a shape that had yet to be revealed. I had not planned it, but there it was, lurking at the edges. One night I dreamed that the world was one infinite house and woke up convinced that if I could finish my work I would grasp the secret that was hidden there. A form would resolve itself into existence, the figure that had been implied all along, although it had nothing to do with what the story appeared to be about.

Since then, I carry on. Some days progress is good, others not. I've learned not to force it. When the work will not come, I walk around the city, not thinking about where I am going. Not long ago I walked all day, and at the end of the afternoon found myself standing on an enclosed pedestrian bridge between a shopping centre and a multistorey car park, watching the people in the street below. I stood for several minutes with my forehead close to the bronze-tinted glass, and then I saw my wife and daughter. They came out of an overground station and waited at the lights, hand in hand. They crossed the road and began to walk along the pavement, passing underneath me. I moved to the other side of the bridge to keep them in sight.

I watched them for as long as I could. I did not know why I was so afraid of losing them in the crowd, or why I was filled with this unexpected joy, this certainty that everything had been worthwhile. My daughter was wearing a plastic raincoat I had not seen before. My wife looked young. They were nowhere near home.

ISAAC

Becca spent the holiday reading and avoiding her cousin. She had brought a bag full of books recommended by one of her English teachers, who said that for the Oxford interview it was important to show she was exploring widely beyond the A-level syllabus. She read *Twelfth Night* in the garden while her father and her uncle tried to set up the hoops on the croquet lawn. When the weather turned bad, halfway into the first week, she read *Villette* on the sofa by the fireplace. Raindrops crawled on the bay window.

Becca's mother had rented the house for a fortnight. It meant a lot to her to bring the family together, because her sister had lived in America for more than twenty years and they did not get to see one another often. Emma and Jack seemed to get on all right with Isaac's younger siblings, the five children sometimes treating one another as invisible and sometimes running as a pack. As for the adults, they were absorbed in themselves: wholly occupied with projects of incredible banality such as preparing large meals, planning outings to National Trust properties and comparing their digital cameras. Becca could not see the appeal of playing at country house living with a family of strangers, but she was content to be left alone with the books.

On Saturday it was fine again, and after breakfast she went to the terrace with *Don Juan*. Within a few minutes she became aware that Isaac was hovering in the French window. This was his habit. Wherever she settled herself, he would appear nearby, shifting his feet, his arms dangling like ropes. Becca had to take great care not to look his way or make any other sign of recognition. It was a balancing act. She must remain poised and composed and very slightly forbidding, but she must not show any hint of superiority. Nothing that could be held against her.

When the clumsiness of his presence became overwhelming, she closed the book and walked back into the house, giving him a brief smile as she passed. He turned after her as if he had something to say, and made a twitching gesture at the book in her hand, but he did not follow. It was unfortunate, but there was no denying that his appearance counted against him. He had the smallest eyes Becca had ever seen, and he thrust his bullet head forward, squinting, as if to compensate for their weakness. His nostrils were slits. When he interrupted her reading she sometimes allowed herself a thrill of horror at his mouth, with its rubbery upper lip that never closed properly over his teeth.

Later, lying on her bed with the book, she heard voices in the sitting room below. Every morning Isaac's father held a sort of prayer-meeting for his family. His voice droned on, with occasional responses from Becca's aunt and cousins. It would continue for at least forty-five minutes, she knew. She could not make out the words, only the drawling southern-states accent that she found hard to take quite seriously. As the meeting went on, his voice grew louder, more rhythmic and emphatic, and the responses became chant-like and excited. By the end, as usual, they were practically whooping.

On the second day of the holiday, Isaac's father had squatted down beside Becca and told her she was welcome to join the family in prayers, any time at all. He sure hoped she'd consider joining them. He was a pastor by profession. He had the same eyes as his son, small and muddy green, but his face was smoothly tanned, and where Isaac was awkward he had a vast self-possession. He did not seem to feel at all out of place. He gripped Becca by the shoulder and stared into her eyes for a long time, as if he were measuring her sincerity against his own. Think about it, he said. She promised that she would.

Becca's mother put her head around the door and told her everyone was getting ready for a walk. Becca said she'd stay behind and get through some more reading. Invigorated by the prospect of having the house to herself for the afternoon, she went downstairs to brew coffee. The fuss of making sandwiches, checking guidebooks and finding walking boots was quite pleasant when you had opted out of it.

As she was setting the pot on the stove, Isaac appeared in the doorway. She had changed over to *Persuasion*, and the book was on the counter beside her, but she could not plausibly pick it up now. She threaded her hair behind her ear.

'You like that, huh?'

She could not tell whether he meant the coffee, the novel, or something else entirely, but she was not going to ask. She smiled noncommittally, and Isaac grinned. He was always grinning for want of a better idea. He rocked forward on the balls of his feet as if he might topple towards her.

Isaac's father came in behind him. He gripped Isaac around the chest with one arm and placed the other hand on the back of his head, scrubbing his skull.

'Hey, boy.'

Isaac convulsed in his father's arms but did not try to escape. He shrank in the embrace, ducking like an animal.

'Forget your manners?'

The pastor took Isaac's head in both hands and planted a kiss on his brow.

'Get on now.'

The pastor gave her a wink as he pushed Isaac from the kitchen.

When the walkers had gone, Becca took her coffee upstairs and finished Austen in the bath. Going through the books, she decided to tackle *The Waves* next. She was surprised at her own appetite for this stuff. It was not just interview prep, she felt. She was bringing something into focus about herself, laying claim to some aspect of the future. She had an inkling that once the holiday was over she would never read in quite the same way again.

The sun was bright, so she took Woolf outside. The house had a large garden which grew unkempt towards the edges and ended at a small pond where, on the first day here, Becca had seen frogs no bigger than her thumbnail. They had been hard to spot in the long grass at the pond's edge, but then she had seen dozens of them at once.

Now she lay down on the well-kept square of lawn behind the house. She ate an apple and threw the core into a flower bed. She had been there for half an hour when a shadow fell on the page. Isaac stood over her, blinking against the light. He grinned and shrugged.

'I stayed behind to reflect,' he said. 'My daddy said I could.'

Becca said nothing. The balancing act was impossible when she was lying propped on one elbow. Carefully, she sat up.

'Those books you read,' he said. 'You won't find your answers there.'

He nodded, agreeing with himself, and gave an abrupt laugh.

'They can only lead you astray.'

There was no point in responding. But looking up at him, standing there, not knowing what to do with his hands, seeming genuinely to believe he had hit on a good way to start a conversation, Becca felt her patience run out.

'Really?' she said. 'Did your daddy tell you that too?'

Again the duck of the head.

'You'll see,' he said. 'You'll get your rightful punishment when our lord and master rises to claim dominion over this world.'

He walked away, stiff-legged.

The next day Isaac was nowhere to be seen, and Becca began to relent. More than anything it was funny. She felt all the advantages she had, and reminded herself of the need to be kind. In his disastrous way he was trying to be friendly – the whole situation must be very foreign to him, after all – and perhaps a little generosity on her part would make a great difference to his life. Perhaps it would be the beginning of the long and painful process by which he might one day overcome his difficulties, and perhaps he himself was dumbly aware that this could happen. That might be the reason he kept hanging around.

When Isaac did not turn up at dinner time, Becca volunteered to go and find him. She went into the garden and circled the house, peering down the paths between the box hedges. The light was losing definition and she found herself looking twice at trees and stone urns, making sure they were only themselves.

She found Isaac at the bottom of the garden, kneeling over the small pond. He had taken his shirt off. His back was muscular, the rope of his spine twisting down to a tuft of blond fur at the rear of his jeans. Becca hesitated, not wanting to intrude. But he was not doing anything, and after a minute she called out that dinner was ready. He looked around just as someone turned on the terrace lamps, and the light fell on his face.

As she walked back to the house, leaving him to his own devices, certain now that whatever he needed was beyond her power to give, she tried to work out how to describe his expression. It was not pain, or anger, or pleasure, or confusion, or shame. He looked like something but she could not think what. She would find the right comparison sixteen years later, immediately after giving birth in a delivery suite in a midwife-led unit in Bristol. Isaac's face would come back to her, if only for the space of a heartbeat, as she looked for the first time at her son: at the umbilical cord wrapped one full turn around his neck, and at the swollen grey-purple face that had not yet crossed over into life. For an instant she would see her cousin's face, groggy with the shock of having been born. She would feel the sensation in her own hand as the midwife forced a thumb under the cord and drew it over the head. She would watch them lift him across to a crash trolley and start rubbing him down, fixing him in the world, coaxing out his first cry.

YOU MUST LEAVE ALL YOUR
BELONGINGS BEHIND

You must go down to the canal at six in the evening. You must walk along the towpath. You must inhale pollen. Look across the canal to the backs of big houses where their gardens trail grass in the water and the boats tug on nylon ropes. The surface moves like oil. You must not think about London. Instead you must scrape the bark and moss as you walk until your fingernails are packed with black. It is warm but it will be cold before dark. You must not let it get too late, but you can keep walking for now. You may hear chatter from a garden close but out of sight. You must not think of those gardens. You must not think about the lives you wanted when you were young. An aeroplane static in the heights is a pale sign as abstract as the moon. You must remember to turn back when you reach halfway. Or perhaps you can walk a little further. You could have brought a jacket but you did not. You must pay attention as the light draws down and the life moves in the brambles, but you must not feel these things too deeply. In these houses they are putting the dinner on, watching the soaps, hearing the news. You must not empty your pockets. You must not take your keys and weigh them in your hand. You must not plan this. If you turned back now you could still be home in time.

ONE-EYED JACK AND THE SUICIDE QUEEN

When I saw her, I was about to leave town. I had been working the saloons for three days and I knew it was time to move on. If I'd followed that instinct I would have saved myself some trouble.

The town, known as Stub to its inhabitants, was bigger than some but no different from most. Packed mud roads, bony mules tied outside the bar rooms, old men sitting in front of their shanties. Any ghostport you like. On the main street the barber nods in his chair, a dog noses at a streak of offal, and bored girls gaze down from a window in hopes of witnessing a fistfight. Months pass, then a crew comes out of the Ghost and the streets fill with traders and middlemen elbowing one another aside to get to the goods, while the scavengers take the coin that's offered them and get to drinking, fornicating and gambling it away. They light bonfires, sing songs for mates who didn't make it home, and cut one another's throats over minor disputes in the early hours of the morning.

Now the town was feverish. Two crews had landed in the space of a week, and I was there to do my part, moving around the edges. Don't stand out, never stay in one place for long. Every joint had its backroom game, and I followed my nose to those that suited me. Not too settled, not too wild. When I was allowed to sit down, I sat down. I did not talk and I never won big.

In my early years there had been times I cleaned out a room in a few hours' steady play. Not hard given the class of game you find in the ghostports, but I had learned what happened next. Win big, they call you a cheat, confiscate your takings and beat you into better manners. One time, in a town further down the perimeter, I schooled a local big noise in five-card stud, and a beating was not enough for him. He had the next inbound crew take me with them and leave me in the purlieus of the Ghost. When I came around I was lying on a slab of smashed tarmac. A metallic rib reached fifty feet above me. Sitting up, I saw uncountable ribs receding, the remains of an infinite beast. I heard a strange cry. As I scrambled to my feet, I caught a glimpse of the horizon – it still comes back to me, that landscape that is no landscape, those impossible monoliths – and I felt my mind falter. I ran and did not stop until I was too exhausted to fear for my sanity any longer.

These days I took no risks. I had done what I could do in Stub, put myself ahead by the usual small margin, and I did not need my face getting familiar in the back rooms. I drank a cup of brown gargle at a street stall, then hefted my knapsack, pulled down the brim of my hat, and started walking.

The main street was a clamour. It would be days yet before the haggling was done. Mostly it was local small-timers risking their funds on scraps of ghostwork that might do anything or nothing, but a good haul always drew its share of interest from further afield, too. This morning the crowd parted here and there for horsemen in the livery of grand houses. One such was moving towards me, seated tall on his glossy black mount. His stirrups were silver and his black curls fell to his shoulders.

I buried my right hand in the folds of my coat. No more proof was needed that I had outstayed my welcome. I picked up my pace, intending to get clear of the town without delay.

Then I saw her.

She was inspecting the wares on a peddler's trestle. I noticed nothing except her face. The light defined her profile. I only saw her for a moment, but that glimpse was enough to fill my heart with confusion. She walked on, and there was nothing for me to do but follow.

She drew attention in the marketplace. She wore a dove-grey travelling cape over a high-throated black dress; her bonnet was black straw and taffeta; she carried a silk valise in the crook of her elbow and held her parasol, folded, in a suede-gloved hand with a pearl button at the wrist. City-made attire, better than the women of Stub could afford, though the hem of the dress was frayed and her boots were splattered with mud. Some of the traders grinned and called, taking her for easy game. She ignored these men or subdued them with a polite remark. Sometimes she inspected an object, but she always moved on without buying.

Her name was Joanna Fortune. She was the last daughter of one of the older houses of Wen, a family rich in history, once wealthy and potent, still proud though long declined from its greatness. I would learn these facts later. For now, all I knew was her face, and as I watched I grew astonished. The resemblance was perfect. Time came undone, and I forgot the thirty-five years that had passed since the festival summer in the city when I had made the mistake that would last me a lifetime.

> • <

Every seventh summer the festival comes to the city of Wen. It came in my eighteenth year and released me from the monotony of my apprenticeship to the Quandrists' Guild. The Quandrists were second to none in the respect and influence they commanded in the city, and they guarded such deep mysteries of the ghostwork that not even the greatest of the noble houses would dare to cross them. So the junior adepts claimed; but every guild held the same opinions about itself. In the four years of my apprenticeship, all the guild had given me was iron rations, rote learning and drudgery in the kitchens. When festival-time came it opened the doors to a kind of freedom I had not known was possible. I left my duties and slipped out to streets where the carnival never flagged.

For the first days of the festival I did nothing but wander through the city, gaping at the puppeteers, fortune-tellers and funambulists who had set their pitches in every plaza. No street corner was without its spectacle, or so it seemed to me. Stilt-walkers scattered handbills announcing all sorts of entertainments. Women wove past costumed in feathers, ribbons, golden wires. They caught my eye, smiled, and flung handfuls of sequins into the air. For the duration of the festivities those sequins were as good as genuine currency. The pretend money somehow made a joke of the real thing, and it seemed only right that pretty women with flushed cheeks could, by throwing bits of glitter into the crowd, make an apprentice as rich as a princeling. It would come to an end, because the festival lasted three months and no longer, but to me three months sounded like forever. I was used to a diet of porridge and sour beer but now my meals were spicy street food. I learned to find the stairways down to the bar rooms and to drink strong wine by the bottle while some satirist pulled faces and shouted until he was drowned out by the band. Awkward as I was, I let myself be drawn into dances by revellers whose names I would never know.

It was in one of those cellar bars that I sat down to my first game of cards. Watching from a distance, I had grown fascinated by the muted theatrics of card-play, and by the invisible tensions that cut the smoky air above the table. I saw that the game's calculations were a matter not just of the figures on the cards but of bluff and counter-bluff, swagger and poise, the secret hopes and fears of every person willing to ante up. Without understanding how, I could see that the players were putting their hearts and souls in question. When I sat down myself, I felt the rules of the game embrace me, drawing me into formalised intimacy with the strangers across the table. When I got up eight hours later and climbed the steps into the dawn, my pockets heavy with sequins, I knew I had discovered a way of life. That's what the game does for you. As long as you're playing, you do not need to understand anything else.

I played every night for a month. For me the cards became a method, a philosophy, a style. When I was not at the table I was always cutting and shuffling a pack. Occasionally I won big, as I had on the first night. When that happened I would nod curtly to the players whose purses I had emptied – I was getting the hang of the game's laconic decorum – and then freewheel through the streets until I found some joint where the night's party was still going strong. I would stand breakfast for everyone, calling for fine liquor, heaping sequins into the hands of whoever wanted them and accepting the cheers and embraces of my new friends as my due. On mornings like that it was impossible to believe the festival could end.

I was still a novice player, of course. I lost more often than I won, and I learned that losing was bitter. I got to know the shame of sitting for hours anteing yourself away on useless hands. I learned that there was no real lesson in it, nothing to muse about as you trailed home: you had lost, and that was all. But there was always the chance that the next game would go better, and it was a certainty that within hours I would be sitting down again. And then some nights I could not lose. I could play as recklessly as I liked, trying my level best to give my money away, and the cards would not let me. At those times, when I was all cunning and charisma at the table, when I played with unthinking generosity and all my optimism turned out to be justified, I knew that I was glimpsing the secret at the heart of the game. If I trusted in the cards they would bless me in return. If I bet with all my courage then the stake I put in the pot would come back to me, marvellously multiplied. I did not often find that state of grace at the card table, but when I did the world made sense and all losses were forgotten.

> • <

I lingered in the streets of Stub for hours, keeping her in sight. I dipped my hat-brim when she turned my way. I wanted nothing in particular, but I did not want the vision to end. When she hitched up her skirts and skipped across a runnel of filth, it was a step that Isabella had once danced on one of the long tables of the Café Selenium. When she paused for a minute's chat with the huge woman who sold counterfeit wares from a stall near the water pump, I knew the tone of voice that Isabella would have used to make the woman laugh as she now did, the mouth gaping to show strong back teeth. The crowds turned envious eyes on the fine city lady but let her pass, wary of what they did not understand.

Much of the town's talk was about an incident last night in which an unlucky broker had mishandled one of his new purchases. According to the gossip, the item had forced its way under his fingernails and begun to transform his body from the inside. Fortunately, a couple of quick-thinking town militia had requisitioned a barrel of rough spirit from the nearest pothouse, doused the mutating thing and set it on fire before any more harm was done. Opinions varied as to what the man had been turning into. As usual after a happening of this sort, there was a jollity in the street chatter and a readiness to start conversations with strangers. I kept my head down. I hung back from the woman, doing my best to look like an idler, moving when she moved. I dared not let my gaze falter for fear I would find her gone.

Someone called my name across the street. It was Pat Shim, an inveterate loser I knew from the hold'em game above one of the big bar rooms on the outskirts of town. He was in difficulty with a couple of local boys, one of whom was gripping his narrow shoulders while the other uncoiled a horsewhip. Shim mugged over at me, all bloodshot eyes and gap teeth, his heels scraping the dirt. He was gabbling about an innocent misunderstanding and that he'd be indebted if I could just help him explain to these gentlemen that his credit was good. Heads turned towards me. I saw her disappearing around a corner. Shim was still bleating my name as I walked on.

I rounded the corner in time to see her enter Monty's. I followed, still unsure of my motives. Maybe I was concerned for the safety of this girl who was so obviously out of place, or maybe I was intrigued by the puzzle of what she was doing here. If these explanations were not wholly false, they were not convincing anyone either.

As I mounted the steps of the saloon my legs weakened under me, and I clung to the rail like an old man, one hand pressed to my sternum. It was a pain I knew, though it had not been this bad for a long time. I leaned on the porch and waited for it to pass.

Isabella, have you forgotten? We were eighteen years old. We ran the length of Avalon Street in the heat of the midsummer night, the Triumphal Arch torch-lit ahead of us like a phantom of the future, the music and roar and stink and perfume of Wen streaming off our bodies and soaking our garments. We were drunk on brandy and dizzy with longing, your hands in my hair, your taste in my mouth, stumbling in the mist of the fountains under the million tiny lights of the festival. Have you forgotten?

Inside Monty's I took up a position at the corner of the bar. I could blend in among the wrecks drinking themselves through the stages to oblivion. I nodded at the barkeep and he poured me a finger of cheap spirit. The windows greased the light. A low-stakes game was in progress at one of the rear tables.

She was seated at the front of the room, arranging her parasol and gloves on a small table set away from the windows. She had her back to me. Opposite her sat a stout man with heavy whiskers, holding his top hat in his lap. The man adjusted the set of his pince-nez. I knew him. His hands, his face, his bald pate and the whites of his eyes were patterned with blue-green fern shapes, fractal markings that he had reputedly gained on a scavenging expedition in his youth. His name was Henry Lipless and now, in his old age, he was one of the town's craftiest fixers. As I watched they reached the end of their discussion, and Lipless laid an object on the table.

She picked it up and manipulated it in some way I could not make out. It was a white cylinder, roughly the size of her forearm. She passed him a roll of notes. His thumb flickered through them and they disappeared into his waistcoat while she slipped the cylinder into her valise. Lipless got to his feet, held his hat to his chest, and bowed as he took his leave. She waited a few minutes before following him out. I knocked my drink back.

She was heading for the worst part of the town. I hurried after: by now I was in no doubt that it was my duty to look out for her. But the back streets were a tangle, and soon I was standing alone among the corrugated-iron shacks, cursing my slowness. I knew these streets and still I had lost her.

Something struck my knee so that I stumbled. I found myself pinned against a wall with a blade under my chin. She asked me who I was and what I wanted. Her irises were warm brown ringed with jade at the edges. Isabella's eyes. The brown curl escaping from her bonnet was Isabella's curl.

'Tell me what they know,' she said.

The blade pressed tighter, and I began to croak that I was nobody, that I knew nothing, that it was all a mistake.

I hardly heard myself. Up close, the resemblance was even stronger. She took the blade away from my throat and stepped back.

'I don't believe you belong to the Trelawneys at all,' she said.

I touched under my jaw and found a smear of blood on my fingertips. The knife was still pointing at my windpipe.

'But you've been following me.'

I shuffled my feet and brushed at the dried mud on one of my coat sleeves. I could not work out how to explain myself. How to begin to put into words that I meant no harm but that I had had no choice, because since seeing her on the main street I no longer understood the difference between a coincidence and a miracle. More than anything, standing there, I was conscious of my appearance: my blotched and sagging face, my grizzled beard and lank grey locks. Down the years I had held on to a trace of secret pride in the figure I cut. I was physically much as I had been at twenty – a little stringier and more slack, but without an ounce more on my frame – and I liked to think that with my beard pointed and my hair tied back with a ribbon, in my duster coat, my old hide hat and my fingerless gloves, I could move through the perimeter towns with a quiet self-sufficiency, a degree of mystery, even a touch of grace. I liked to think I wore the eyepatch like a badge of hard-bought wisdom. Now those notions fell away and I stood in front of her like a shabby old man.

'I wanted to help you,' I said. 'Make sure you were safe.'

She studied me, and reached a decision. She sheathed the blade and gave it a twist so that the weapon was gone and her parasol was whole again. She made a mocking curtsey.

'Then accept my thanks, kind sir. I assure you I require no further assistance.'

I stood there, slow on the uptake. Then, grasping that I was free to go, I tugged down the brim of my hat and began to walk away.

I had taken several steps before I noticed that the alley ahead of me was blocked at the far end by three men. They were in leather riding-gear, their jerkins quartered black and silver, swords drawn. I looked back. More men were approaching from the other end of the alley.

She smiled, and I had to remind myself yet again that she was not Isabella.

'These gentlemen, on the other hand,' she said, '*they* work for the Trelawneys.'

> • <

Five weeks into the festival, in a little attic café overlooking the Dew Street Gardens, I sat down to a game that ran through the night and into the next day. There had been six players to begin with, but by mid-morning it was down to me and a young man who wore two silver rings on each hand and kept his face placid behind a neat black beard. We did not know one another's names, but we knew that between us we had driven the weaker players out. We had barely spoken, but we had been conversing for hours in the language of bets and bluffs. Eventually he turned over ace-queen, I turned over ace-king, and I raked in the last of his sequins. He gave a rueful whistle. He asked if I'd treat him to a nice plump capon: he was starving.

When we had eaten we fell to talking, and soon we were strolling together through the Botanical Quarter. We were old hands at the festival, unruffled by the touts and hawkers. His name was Erik and he was the second son of a great house. I had never spoken on equal terms with a noble before, but it did not feel strange.

We came to an old palazzo, and he led me up the staircase to a run-down ballroom where a group of young people were rehearsing a play. They wore the bright rags that many revellers favoured in festival time, but I knew at once that they were nobility too. I steadied myself to meet their eyes. The black-bearded youth was confessing that he had an ulterior motive for bringing me to meet his friends. Their Pedrolino had fallen off a balcony drunk the night before last, and was now home in bed with a bandage around his stupid skull. Their first performance was tomorrow, and the costume would fit me perfectly...

I had never acted in a play and I had no wish to, but I was already nodding. The young nobles cheered, slapped my shoulders and kissed my cheeks, but I barely noticed, because I had seen the woman sitting at the spinet on the far side of the room. I had seen her, and now I could see nothing else. Her hands rested on the keyboard. Brown curls framed her face and there was a promise of laughter in the set of her lips. Her lashes flickered, but she was not taking her eyes away from mine.

Trust the cards, I was telling myself. Bet bold.

In the back streets of Stub, the young woman who looked like my Isabella watched the men approach from the ends of the alley. She gripped the haft of her parasol. I grabbed her wrist and pulled her between two shanties. We scrambled under a wire fence, ducked through a section of rusted pipe, and paused in the wreck of a long-abandoned shack.

'I know my way around,' I gasped.

She gave me a doubtful look, but I was in the grip of an optimism I had not felt for decades, my lungs raw and my heart hammering. We could hear the faint shouts of the men lost in the shantytown.

An hour later Stub was behind us. The trail we had taken ran into the purlieus: her choice, because it meant a smaller chance of being followed. She set a fast pace and I had little breath to spare.

At sundown we made camp in the lee of a ruin from the old times. Resting our backs against a pink stone buttress of inexplicable size, we shared provisions. I gave her a strip of dried pork from my knapsack. She produced a slab of something hard and white wrapped in waxed paper, which, when I popped a fragment into my mouth, was so intensely sweet that I almost choked. As it softened on my tongue I felt new vigour trickling into my limbs. We swigged water from my canteen and watched the campfire.

I murmured the name she had told me – *Joanna Fortune* – as if to persuade myself that this really was not Isabella, this young woman taking her ease in the borderlands of the Ghost as coolly as if she were sitting in an ice cream parlour by the Grand Canal.

She was on the run from agents of some powerful house in Wen. That much was obvious. My reward for thirty-five years spent wandering the borderlands was that I knew the dirt roads and hopeless townships better than any gang of hunters from the city. As the fire settled in its embers, I made plans. We would skirt the Ghost as far as Heaptown, then make for smaller ports like Slickside, Pitmire and Sty. I watched her face in the firelight. I would be her guide and protector, I thought. We would keep to the edges and keep moving, and her pursuers would never catch us.

When I put this to her she shook her head. She wasn't for running or hiding, she told me: she was going back to Wen.

'So you know your way around,' she said. 'That's worth something.'

She gave me one of Isabella's smiles.

'Get me there within the week, it's worth a ducat.'

I laughed, then started coughing. When I could breathe again, I lifted my right hand and pulled up the glove far enough to show the brand on the ball of my thumb.

'Wen's not for me,' I said.

Joanna moved to the far side of the fire and lay down with her parasol in her hand, settling her head on her valise. I stretched my legs out, groaned, and made myself as comfortable as I could for the first watch of the night. The sky was glassy dark. Somewhere behind us a flicker of cold light rose from the Ghost, snaked to the zenith and disappeared. I took out a deck of cards and began to deal stud hands.

I woke at dawn to find the ashes of the fire kicked over and Joanna gone. My chest tightened around the old pain; but as I sat up she appeared from behind a section of shattered wall, smoothing down her skirts. She shouldered her valise and made a curtsey.

I watched her walk away, heading in the direction that would lead her back to the city where my life was forfeit to the House of Montresor. So it goes, I said to myself. I would press on to Heaptown, maybe find a seat in the back room at Yardley's where they ran a tight game of five-card draw, Jacks or better. I would not stay long or stand out. I would not win big.

Joanna crested the rise against the dawn sky. In another moment she would be out of sight. I scrambled to my feet, got my knapsack together and set off after her, ignoring the stiffness in my knees and back, calling out as I staggered forward: calling that I had changed my mind, calling for her to slow down, calling for her not to go without me.

> • <

Her name was Isabella Damson. She was gentry, the only daughter of a good family, and blessed with personal merits enough to make her welcome in circles even better than her own. She and her friends were occupying the old palazzo for the duration of the festival – it was the disused property of someone's generous or careless relation – and they lived there as a tribe of the carefree young, picnicking in the empty parlours, chasing along the hallways in their bright rags, smoking rare weeds and philosophising all night in the library, strolling half-clad in and out of the huge gothic bathrooms and trading their places in the many bedrooms of the house as often as the whims of their hearts required.

In this setting I would have been crippled with shyness if I had had the attention to spare. But I had Isabella to think about. After the play's last performance we all ended up back at the palazzo, toasting our triumph with pale gold brandy. Someone had found dozens of the slim-necked bottles in the cellar, and someone else had lit the candelabras in the ballroom so that we reeled like planets among our blazing constellations. I had known them for a matter of days but I had never loved anyone half so well. A lacquered cabinet turned out to contain a ghostwork mechanism that filled the house with music, throbbing and lachrymose, thrillingly loud. The night swelled with laughter and body heat and the tang of the brandy, until at last I noticed that the music had stopped and everyone else had passed out on the sofas or vanished into other parts of the house. Everyone except Isabella, who was sitting on a love-seat in front of a tall window where the dawn was beginning to show. She was waiting. I seemed to cross the whole length of the room in a stride.

I woke in bright sunshine, alone, fully dressed, my legs hanging over one end of the love-seat, my head a slow carousel. I stumbled to the nearest privy to be sick in the bowl, then ran my head under the pipe and began to explore the palazzo. The innocent hush of revellers sleeping off a party. I found Isabella brewing coffee in the downstairs kitchen. She had already set two small blue cups on the table. She poured, and pushed one towards me. It was as if we had reached some agreement last night. If I could not remember what it was, I did not mind, because without further discussion we now set out to explore the festival together. We gave Wen to one another like a gift: its parks and riverboats, its open-air concerts and midnight burlesque shows. Several times each day we parted for the pleasure of meeting again. When we met our hands would entangle and she would lift her face to mine. One night we stood in the mist of the fountains on Avalon Street and I pulled her close to me, smiling as I murmured against her cheek, knowing that her blood was fizzing with the same excitement as my own.

When she drew away from me I felt a lurch in the chest that I recognised. It was the lurch that comes when you've misplayed a hand, raised the pot only to find that your cards are not as strong as you thought. I hardly knew what I had been saying – blandishments and persuasions, plans for the night and for many nights to come – but I knew at once that none of it would come to pass. You feel the game get away from you even as you place the bad bet, long before you understand the mistake you've made. In some secret part of myself I was not surprised when she told me she was engaged to be married to Zachary Montresor, eldest son of the great and noble House of Montresor, in two weeks' time, on the last day of the festival.

> • <

We made for Wen, finding our path through the penumbra of the Ghost, sometimes walking the old roads and sometimes the trails of recent time. We kept clear of settlements, stopping only once to fill our canteens at a clean spring I knew. We saw no one until noon of the second day, when a group of mounted figures appeared on the ghostward horizon. They would overtake us within the hour, and if they meant mischief there was no help for it, no way to run or hide. We kept walking.

As they drew nearer I counted six riders. The mounts were stalking-pigs, heavy-headed, their tusks and snouts huge. The animals blundered forward with the unsteady gait that made the elongated legs seem always about to collapse under the fleshy bodies. The riders themselves were tricked out in a certain borderland style: naked except for scraps of leather and chain, their torsos scarified and daubed with red mud, their heads half-shaved and sprouting locks like matted ropes, their faces pierced with studs, bolts and plates. They carried spiked maces, serrated lances and metal whips, and wore bunches of dried skulls at their waists.

As they encircled us they rolled their eyes, drew back their lips to show filed teeth and waggled their tongues suggestively. I sighed. Joanna was reaching into her valise, but a whip slashed it to the ground. One of the riders dismounted and scooped it up. He looked Joanna over appreciatively, then chuckled at me.

For the rest of the day we walked at the rear of the gang with our hands tied behind our backs. Ropes ran from the saddle of one of the stalking-pigs to make nooses around our necks. The riders whooped and bellowed.

'Who are they?'

I shrugged, and almost stumbled.

'Some cult.'

'Where are they taking us?'

I said nothing. She already knew the answer that counted, and I did not care to say it out loud. They were taking us towards the Ghost. We were a way off the true interface, but already my skin was prickling and the air had a viscid quality on my face and throat; just imagination or something real, I could not tell.

At nightfall our captors led us into an enormous yard where a great bonfire blazed, the firelight gleaming on the wet limbs of cultists and on the blades of cleavers and knives. The yard was overshadowed by a squat, cliff-like building of ancient times. Fires flickered in the windows. Some of the cultists were beating iron poles on metal barrels while others cavorted to the rhythm. To my mind, inviting so much attention so near the Ghost was a gamble no one needed to take.

A howl went up when they saw us. They dragged us to a place where big iron hoops were fixed into the ground. Two men secured us by the wrists while other cultists moved nearer.

'I need my bag,' Joanna said.

There were at least two dozen cultists, men and women, all pierced and scarified and trussed in straps and spikes. One of them stepped forward: a huge man, tall and heavy, wearing a headdress like a bull's horns. Sweat coated his face and his belly, and a giant leather phallus bobbed at his crotch. His right hand was missing but in its place he wore a ghostwork claw, its three ceramic fingers long and scalpel-sharp.

He bared the whites of his eyes.

'My children,' he boomed. 'My lost children. You are the children of the Bull now.'

As he spoke, telling us to give up all hope and abandon ourselves to horror because our future held only lingering torment and agonising demise, I tried to think who he reminded me of. Then I worked it out. He was like one of Isabella's actor friends, the one who had played the lead in that festival show. This man had the same bully swagger and stagey delivery.

'As you scream, my children, as you learn the degradation to which the flesh can be forced, know this: your suffering has no purpose but the pleasure of the Bull.'

Three female cultists gathered around him, caressing his hairy biceps. They pursed their lips and struck awkward poses, doll-like and parodic. They pretended to laugh, watching Joanna as if anxious to gauge the effect they were having.

'Nothing is real but horror!' bawled the huge man, and all the cultists shrieked happily in response. 'Nothing is real but the pleasures of the Bull!'

I peered into the darkness beyond the bonfire. Something was moving out there, at the edges of the yard.

The leader grinned, showing long, blackened teeth sharpened to points. I could hear from the man's accent that he had been born and raised in Wen, and the north side at that. I saw a gleam of firelight on something pallid that darted out of view, and I heard a new noise behind the drumming and the shrieks: a slithering, rustling muttering that swelled on every side of the yard at once.

The huge man put his face close to Joanna's.

'We shall feast on you now, my pretty child,' he said. 'We shall enjoy you down to the last joint and use you up to the last morsel.'

Two cultists cut Joanna loose and dragged her towards the bonfire. The leader spat phlegm on the sleeve of my coat.

'The hogs can have this one.'

Joanna struggled in the grip of the cultists but could not break free. They twisted her to face the leader. He flexed his claw.

Something came forward into the circle of firelight. It looked like a face, chubby and cherubic, but it was as large as a grown man's torso. It paused, smiling toothlessly, then lunged on the nearest cultist.

Creatures swarmed into the yard. They were pig-like things with the limbs of millipedes and the faces of giant human babies. The one that had fixed itself to the cultist began to suck out the screaming man's innards. Within a few seconds the same was happening all around us.

I tugged at my bonds. Joanna broke away from her panicking captors and moved through the chaos, quick and calm, dodging terrified cultists and stalking-pigs. She sidestepped one of the ghost-things as it rose from its meal. It belched and a slick thighbone slipped from its mouth.

I lost sight of her as she passed behind the bonfire, but she reappeared with her valise on her shoulder. She was holding the white cylinder she had bought from Henry Lipless, and I could have sworn that now the creatures shied away from her as she strode through the yard.

The cultists' leader blocked her path. He was wild-eyed and laughing as if he welcomed the carnage. His claw was dripping with dark fluid, and he gripped a wet meat-hook in his hand. He and Joanna circled one another.

When he grabbed for her, she made a single dancer's gesture. Opening the white cylinder to reveal that it was the scabbard for a short sword, she stepped neatly in and brought the blade down to sever the man's left arm at the shoulder.

The limb hit the ground. It could have been a trick of the firelight that made it seem to start crawling away, dragging itself by the fingers. Joanna swept the sword upward and amputated the leader's other arm. He looked surprised. No blood fell from his wounds.

The third stroke of Joanna's blade took off his head, which bounced on the surface of the yard and came to rest on its side. Its mouth moved and its eyes flicked around in confusion. The leader's torso was still standing in front of Joanna. It swayed, then sat down.

The ropes on my wrists sprang apart when she touched them with the blade.

'This way,' she said, handing me my knapsack.

We walked into the darkness, leaving behind the glow of the bonfire, the screams of the cultists and the kissing sounds that the ghost-things made as they fed. I took a deck of cards from my pocket and began to cut and shuffle as I walked.

> • <

With the festival in its final week, the streets of Wen grew yet more colourful and crowded, the city ever more feverish in its celebrations. As for me, I slept the days away and played poker by night in underground rooms. By now sequins were hard to come by and my funds were running low, but still I found comfort in the fact that I was losing heavily every time I sat down. It seemed fitting. The House of Montresor was rich and ruthless on a scale inconceivable to the likes of me, and if Isabella was destined for such greatness then it had all been a mistake. Somehow I had deluded myself that I was of interest to her when in truth I had been a stricken puppy following her around. It did not bear thinking about, so instead I shuffled the cards and anted up.

One night I found myself facing Erik across the table. We played until dawn, then walked along the Grand Canal. Uneasy with silence, I asked after his friends, and he told me a couple of their misadventures. I did not listen. He mentioned that Isabella was now lodged on the Montresor estate in the north of the city. She would be staying there, making her preparations, until the day of the wedding.

We leaned on the parapet and watched the still surface of the water.

'There's a private game at the Bronze Head,' he said. 'Seven-card stud, straight up. I'll get you an invite.'

I shook my head.

'Tonight cleaned me out.' I touched my empty pockets. 'Didn't have the cards.'

The last gondola of the night slid past below. Erik stroked his beard, which had grown more raffish over the weeks of the festival. He clapped me on the shoulder and turned to go.

'You had the cards,' he said, looking back at me. 'You just weren't betting like you wanted the pot.'

Those words spoke themselves over and over in my mind that day, as I walked away from the heaving heart of Wen and through the avenues of large, clean, solid houses that spread into the northern part of the city. In those spacious neighbourhoods the festival was no more than a hum of music in the distance.

On a tree-lined street I found a wall of white stone more than twice my height. It ran unbroken as far as I could see in both directions. I walked, keeping the wall on my left hand, and after a while I passed a small door of stout oak. Later I came to heavy iron gates that barred the entrance to a long driveway and a prospect of landscaped parkland. The Montresor estate. Beside the gates, a desiccated corpse crouched in the cage of a gibbet. It took me almost two hours to circle the wall back to the place where I had begun.

I wandered through the New Town as the sky began to turn violet. I found a little money in my pocket, not a festive sequin but a real copper coin, and swapped it for a glass of brandy in a café. The well-dressed old men at the other tables frowned, but the proprietress, a motherly woman with a beauty spot in her bosom, smiled at me and gave me a honey cake for nothing.

If you're going to play, I said to myself, bet like you mean it.

Evening came on. I waited under a tree beside the high white wall. Once it was dark enough I shinned up the trunk and climbed along a branch. It swayed and bounced, and for a minute or two all my schemes were reduced to the need not to fall twenty feet onto paving stones. But I inched over the top of the wall, and lowered myself until I was hanging by my fingertips. I dropped to the ground and got up, my ankles throbbing.

I was looking across a miniature hilly landscape decorated with artificial lakes and stands of trees. In the middle distance an enormous house stood dark against the last of the sunset. Nothing moved. Ducking low, I crossed the open park and stole through a formal garden. A hundred windows looked down on me, a few lights flickering behind the panes. I had half-expected all kinds of hazards inside the estate – watchmen, guard dogs, traps – but I had not anticipated the sheer size of the place, or its desertion. It seemed a sort of mockery. I could stumble around out here all night and never get any closer.

Then I heard music. A spinet on which someone picked out a phrase once, twice, three times. I saw a pair of glass doors standing open, spilling light across a stone terrace. I crept closer as the music ceased. Her room was lit by a single lamp, the warm gleam falling on a satin sofa, a velvet hanging and a still life in oils. She hurried over and pulled me inside.

'What do you want?'

We would leave right now, I told her. We would find a way out of this place and by morning be far away. Perhaps we would be running for the rest of our lives, but that would not matter, because we would be together. I told her I didn't blame her for getting mixed up with the Montresors. I saw that she needed to know I would not give her up, no matter what obstacles stood in my way. She needed me to prove I was ready to fight for her.

Her dark curls fell to shoulders clad in green satin. The lamplight gleamed in the darkness of her eyes, and I knew that my own eyes were bright with the same light. I was finding the courage I had lost in all those losing games. It was obvious now. You get the cards you need when you bet like you deserve them.

She gave her head a tiny shake.

'Go away,' she said. 'You must never come here.'

After that, my memories of the night are muddled. I remember how my voice grew loud as I told her she didn't know what she was saying. I accused her of lying and deceit. I remember how I reached for her, as if by holding tightly enough I could convince her of the truth, and how she pushed me away and called for help. I bumped a table and sent a samovar crashing to the floor, and the room seemed immediately to fill with men who pulled me away from her and struck me with their fists until there was nothing else to remember.

When day broke I was in the centre of a great courtyard. My head and hands were trapped in a pillory. The iron compressed my throat. I heard laughter and subdued argument, and the clink of metal. Eventually someone strolled into my field of view. He was a man of my own age, tall and broad, with heavy leonine features, an imperial moustache and blond hair in a thick braid. He wore a quilted purple gown. He leant down to look into my eyes.

'Come,' he said, beckoning to someone I could not see. Isabella appeared, looking solemn, and he put his arm around her waist.

'A common boy makes an attempt on the honour of my wife-to-be,' said the man. 'What am I to do about this?'

I struggled to focus on his face. He had pale blue eyes.

'Usually such a one could expect to live out the short time remaining to him in a certain chamber beneath this house. And I'd instruct Mister Fell, here, to make that short time most exceedingly unpleasant.'

Someone else moved into view: a grizzled old man in a leather apron, dragging a small, wheeled brazier. The heat of it touched my face. He grimaced at Zachary Montresor, then turned his attention to tending the coals.

'Luckily for you, my wife-to-be has a tender heart, and she knows exactly how to put me in a good mood.'

The hand resting on her waist moved lower and squeezed. The betrothed couple locked eyes for a moment and exchanged a private smile.

'She's persuaded me that in your case the fitting punishment is exile.'

I had insulted the House of Montresor, he told me, so henceforth I would bear the brand of Montresor. If I was found within the city walls after sunset today my life would be forfeit. Such a sentence was in the power of a great house to impose.

'Frankly, I find it crueller,' Montresor said. 'All the time you'll have to think about your life.'

The old man called Fell stirred the brazier. When he drew the iron from the coals its end was glowing. I hauled at the pillory with all my strength. I tried to say Isabella's name but began to cough instead.

'One moment, if you please, Mister Fell,' said Montresor.

He took an object from his gown. It was a short brass cylinder like a pocket spyglass. He admired it, running a finger across the intricate chasing of its surface.

'Fascinating piece, this,' he said.

He unscrewed a cap at one end of the cylinder. Isabella began to say something, but he raised a hand.

'I've never tried it on a human being. Couldn't forgive myself if I missed the chance.'

He placed the open end of the cylinder over my left eye. I thought I saw a burst of sparks. Then all the eye could see was darkness. When he moved away from me, replacing the cap on the device and slipping it back into his pocket, the darkness remained. There was no pain, no shock or damage. My left eye's vision had simply been scooped away.

Montresor peered into my face.

'Yes, look,' he said. 'Fascinating.'

He turned to Isabella.

'Now, now, none of that. You'll make me jealous.'

With half my eyesight gone my head felt strange. All my perceptions were twisted out of true. Montresor gave a signal to his minion and the old man came forward with the branding iron.

> • <

Joanna Fortune handed me a note to the value of one ducat, wished me a safe journey, and walked away.

I had not been this close to Wen in thirty-five years. From here a broad stretch of ancient highway ran straight to the city. Three hours' walk would bring a traveller to the gates. I had done as she asked and had got my reward, and there was no reason for me to go any further. I would rest a short while, I decided, then start back for the ghostports. I could reach Jawbone by tomorrow night.

I climbed steps to what must once have been a footbridge across the highway. Now only a stump of concrete reached into space, wrapped in ivy. It made a good vantage point, so I settled with my back against the railing and chewed a piece of biscuit. I eased off my boot to examine a blister on my heel. I took out my needle and thread and repaired a button that had worked loose on my waistcoat. The wide, level surface of the highway was coated in springy grass and wild flowers. I could still see Joanna, but she was a tiny figure by now, coming in and out of view as she passed slabs of overgrown debris and the shells of ancient vehicles.

I stowed my sewing kit, laced up my boot, and hoisted my knapsack onto my back. Then I shook my head and cursed under my breath. Standing at the parapet of the broken bridge, I called Joanna's name. I climbed down and followed her.

I walked until my knees were aching. I was breaking the rules that had kept me in one piece all these years. Don't bet too bold, don't try for the big pot, don't call attention to yourself. I could not help it. I was not ready to go back to the same old wanderings, playing for the same low stakes for the years I had left. Something else had started to happen. Guide, guardian, retainer: it was a role I was getting to like.

At length I reached a place where the remains of an ancient juggernaut lay across the road, the great skeleton of rust showing through the pelt of moss and grasses. I found a ladder on the side and climbed up for a vantage point. The road ahead was deserted. I could not understand how I had lost her.

As I climbed down she stepped in front of me, drawing her sword. She pointed it at my chest and moved closer until I was backed against the wreck.

'Why are you still here?'

The blade was an ugly object, a couple of hands long, slightly curved, slate-grey.

'I've changed my mind about you,' she said. 'You may not be working for the Trelawneys, but you have ideas of your own.'

I shook my head.

'Give me a reason you keep following,' Joanna said, 'or I try this thing again.'

The tip of the blade was an inch away. She touched it to the front of my waistcoat, and I felt a numbing vibration in the spot.

'All right,' I said. 'All right.'

Telling the story took a few minutes. When I had finished I was weak as a baby. I sank down by the old machine and unscrewed my canteen with trembling hands. Joanna sheathed her sword. She had listened to my story with her lips pressed together and a frown creasing her brow, but now her restraint failed, and she laughed.

'I remind you of her,' Joanna said. 'So you want to come with me though your life is forfeit in Wen. You want to help me though you have no idea what I'm going to do. Just because I remind you of someone, you're going to follow me blindly and do whatever I ask.'

She was amused.

'That's what you're asking me to believe?'

I said nothing. I stowed my canteen and began to get up. My legs were shaky but I held myself together with all my wounded dignity. I did not especially care, I felt, whether she let me slink back to the borderlands or put an end to me here. I shouldered my knapsack and turned away.

'Jack,' she called.

I looked back. She beckoned me towards the city.

'Come on, then.'

> • <

The Fortunes were one of the minor noble families of Wen: honourable in their history, comfortable in their circumstances, and content to take no part in the quarrels and conspiracies of the greater houses. Joanna and her brother Marcus had grown up with every advantage, accustomed to every happiness, doted on by parents who were always kind but never indulgent, parents who taught them the responsibilities that came with privilege and made sure they were well-trained in every civilised art from rhetoric to swordplay, medicine to mathematics. Throughout childhood Joanna and Marcus knew only the simplest forms of the ghostwork. Their parents were rationalists above all, and believed in self-reliance.

Alas, the Fortunes caught the attention of the House of Trelawney. The Trelawneys were ten times richer than the Fortunes and a hundred times more ambitious, but they could trace their ancestry only a fraction as far into the city's past. Cassius and Bianca, patriarch and matriarch of the Trelawneys, envied that pedigree and wanted it for themselves. They decided that their younger son Dion must marry Joanna Fortune.

When the Trelawneys set their hearts on a prize they would have it no matter what. But Joanna knew she would sooner die than marry into that family. Dion and his brother Orlando took to arriving unannounced at the Fortunes' house in absurd pomp, riding on white horses in gilded harness, accompanied by squads of guardsmen and troupes of dancers. The Trelawney brothers, got up like a pair of peacocks, would push past the Fortunes' servants, and Orlando's lip would curl at the modest size of the entrance hall and the shabbiness of the tapestries. As for Dion, his tongue would lie wet and heavy on his lower lip as his eyes crawled over Joanna herself. She would have to listen as Orlando delivered his brother's suit in an elaborate speech, his voice dripping sarcasm, while Dion himself stood staring at her and picking his nose.

On their third visit, Joanna and Marcus sent the pair on their way before they could begin the performance. That day her parents sent a formal letter to the House of Trelawney indicating that their daughter was not for the suit, that this was the final word on the matter, and that no further importunities would be heard.

Nothing happened for a fortnight. Then one warm evening Joanna's parents went for a stroll in their garden. They were found in the early hours of the following morning, lying in their favourite arbour with their throats cut. The city watch could find no evidence of the killer, and quickly concluded that the crime was the work of an intruder who had scaled the garden wall in hopes of committing a robbery. This in spite of the fact that the victims' matching gold chains lay undisturbed on their bloody breasts.

Joanna warned her brother that they must be cautious and clever if they were to expose the Trelawneys, but Marcus would not listen. That night he confronted Orlando and Dion Trelawney in the dining room of the Hyperion, accused them of murder, and called each of them out to a duel. The Trelawneys accepted the challenge. Orlando proposed a meeting at dawn in the field at Riverturn: the weapons would be rapier and dagger, and the bouts would be fought consecutively, with the challenger first engaging the elder Trelawney and then, should he live, proceeding to settle his score with Dion. Marcus agreed to these terms, and set out the following morning in spite of Joanna's protests.

He was halfway to the duelling field when he was ambushed by a gang of men who knocked him to the ground and trapped him in what seemed to be a net. It was ghostwork, woven from a substance like fine wire, and when it fell on Marcus it clung to him, contracted around his body, and began to burn. Within a minute he was a corpse, but the net continued to shrink and sizzle until nothing was left but a bundle of sticks and a blackened skull. Both of Marcus's seconds were knifed by the assailants, but one survived to bring the remains home to Joanna.

She left the city that day.

This was the story Joanna told me as we walked the last stretch of the highway and came within sight of the city walls. If I was going to help her, she said, I ought to know. This was why she had travelled into the ghostports and acquired a curious weapon at an exorbitant cost, this was why the Trelawneys were hunting for her, and this was why she was returning to the city. She was going to take her revenge.

We entered Wen by the Tunnel Gate, Joanna using a mixture of charm, hauteur and bribery to ease us through unchallenged. I walked a step behind her, keeping my head down, but soon I was gaping at the spectacle of the city. I saw clouds of brightly coloured pigment rising above rooftops and rolling down into the streets; I heard a drum roll and a cymbal clash, and the cheers of a crowd; I smelled hot cider and onions frying in butter. Someone wearing a grinning pasteboard mask grabbed my hand and shook it, and when I looked I found a gold sequin in my palm.

'Didn't you know?' Joanna said. 'It's festival time.'

> • <

The Fortunes' house was in Summerside, a handsome old palazzo at the end of a quiet avenue where willows brushed the pavement. The front door opened with a push. I followed Joanna into a gloomy hallway.

She lit a lamp. Hangings had been torn from the walls, and a grandfather clock lay on its side, its face smashed. The marble floor was strewn with fragments of porcelain and glass. A faint, foul smell hung in the air.

We moved through well-proportioned rooms, all in disarray. The wreck of a crystal chandelier rested on the dining table. Books had been torn from the library shelves and the shelves themselves kicked apart. Every pane in the conservatory was broken. Joanna said nothing. As we started up the main staircase she gave a cry and hastened to the landing. Following, I found her kneeling beside a corpse.

'It's Beni,' she said.

The dead youth was dressed in a servant's livery. He had been here several weeks, by the looks of it. My guess was that a blow to the head had been the end of him.

We searched the rest of the house. In an attic room we found a second body, similarly decayed, which Joanna told me was that of her father's valet. He had been murdered in his bed.

Joanna stood at the window and looked down into her family's garden. Then we both started at the sound of a crash somewhere in the house below us. Joanna drew the ghostwork sword.

We cornered the intruder in the kitchens. A ragged woman was going through a cupboard, pulling down jars of preserves and stuffing them into a cloth bag. When Joanna grabbed her shoulder, she cringed. Her clothes were filthy, I saw, and her face had been ruined by time and hardship.

'Just looking,' she whined, sinking to the floor in front of Joanna. 'No harm.'

The place had been like this for many weeks, the trampwoman explained. It was rumoured that the Fortunes had incurred the disfavour of a great house, and had paid the price. No one liked to name the house in question, but one night, it was said, that house had sent its men to the home of the Fortunes to smash and pillage, driving out the servants and killing those who could not get away. No one knew what had become of the family themselves – the father and mother, the son and the daughter – but none doubted they were dead or worse.

'Fine, decent folk, I hear,' said the trampwoman, pursing her mouth tragically. 'Not right on them.'

Joanna held the ghostwork weapon at her side, unsheathed. The tendons showed in her knuckles.

'Out,' she said.

The trampwoman scrambled out of the kitchen, dropping her bag. Jars rolled across the flagstones.

Joanna shifted her grip on the haft of her sword. The kitchens were a cavernous warren under the house, with black iron ovens, deep dim larders and long oak boards. Cold emanated from the stone walls. Cured joints and bulbous vegetables hung from hooks in the ceiling. Something moved in the corner of my eye, and I saw a black rat nosing along the countertop.

Without looking, Joanna lashed the sword sideways. The rat fell to the floor, sliced in half. There was no blood, and both parts of the body were still moving, the rear half curling its tail and scrabbling its legs while the front, a few feet away, pulled itself along with its paws. The head ranged around, puzzled.

Joanna sheathed the sword and walked out of the kitchen. I lifted the poker from the fireplace. I bent over the strangely animate pieces of the rat, took aim at the head, and struck a single blow. Both parts convulsed at once and stopped moving.

When I caught up with Joanna she was at the top of the main staircase, wrapping the remains of the messenger boy in a linen sheet. She folded the stiff white fabric over his face and smoothed it with a gentle hand.

'First we bury my servants.'

> • <

From Summerside I walked a mile along the river, crossed at the Heron Bridge, and cut through Eastlight towards the central piazzas where the festival was raucous. I was dressed in bright rags and a domino mask, and I even carried a striped wand decorated with ribbons and bells, but it was an effort to keep up the carefree manner that my outfit demanded. I kept tripping on kerbstones and losing my way. Dray-horses and gangs of revellers barrelled across my path. I could not recall the city being half so crowded the last time I was here.

Night was falling, and many of the festivalgoers carried lanterns and torches. A chain of drunken boys and girls, dancing past with their arms linked, cheered as if I was someone they knew. One of them caught my hand and pulled me in their wake. I played along, jingling my wand, and broke away as soon as I could.

The Mirrored Room Cabaret was hidden in one of the alleys beyond Avalon Street. It had had a reputation in my day, and it was still going strong. The night was young but already the place was heaving with blades, dandies, rakes and libertines, all bent on debauchery. Sweet smoke, liquor bottles, roars of agony and joy at the roulette table, throbbing beats and slewing melodies from the Nuevo Tango combo on stage, the corseted waists and powdered flesh of the women: the Mirrored Room would be the envy of every ghostport dive I had passed through in thirty-five years. As for me, I hung behind a gilded pillar and wished I was anywhere else.

It was not hard to identify the Trelawney brothers. They were holding court at the largest table, surrounded by sycophants and half-dressed young women. One of the brothers – Dion, from his wet grin – had a woman perched on his lap. Her black hair was secured with a dozen diamond pins, and she was laughing convincingly at everything the Trelawneys said. As I watched, Dion shoved her to the floor, then grabbed a bottle and flung it across the table. It shattered against the wall. His face was twisted with fury, and it looked as though worse violence might follow, but instead Orlando said something to his brother and the whole party guffawed. As the black-haired woman was getting up, Orlando's boot prodded her in the behind so that she sprawled on her hands and knees. She blushed and giggled and wagged a finger at him, then tottered away.

At the bar I opened Joanna's purse and paid an exorbitant amount for a bottle of brandy whose label showed a serpent being crushed by a foot while fixing its fangs in the heel: the Trelawneys' favourite, I knew. Armed with this, I jingled my way over to their table.

I found myself slipping into a manner that was not my own. I capered and bowed my way towards them, offering the brandy bottle in a pantomime of servility. Dion grabbed the bottle and smashed the neck on the edge of the table. He upended it and drank, the spirit running down his chin. When the bottle was three-quarters empty, Orlando snatched it from him and sloshed the remainder into a goblet.

'You've got taste in liquor, old clown,' he said. Then he was on his feet, grabbing me by the back of the neck and forcing the goblet into my mouth. I spluttered and swallowed, and Orlando shoved me into a chair.

'My brother has a trusting nature,' he said, his lip curling. 'But I don't like gifts from strangers.'

He tossed the goblet over his shoulder.

'What do you want?'

It was easy to play the part I had chosen; easy to wring my hands and offer a lickspittle smile as I implored them to believe that I only wanted to present my humble services, and that I would never have dared to impose on their valuable time were it not that I happened to be in possession of a certain piece of information which I had reason to suppose might be of considerable interest to their famous and noble selves.

Dion was not listening. He pulled a knife from his boot and checked his reflection in the blade. But Orlando's eyes narrowed as I promised to lead them to someone they wanted.

'Who?'

A few minutes later we were walking towards Summerside. I had gained the attention of both brothers by telling them that I was the servant of Joanna Fortune, and that she had come back to Wen. She had fled the city and had been wandering the borderlands, I explained, but by now her condition was so desperate that she had decided to risk the journey home, hoping to recover a few small items of value.

She was terrified they would catch her, I said, as we pushed through the throng on the Heron Bridge. She had barely had the nerve to creep back to her house, and she would not dare stay any longer than she had to. Within the hour she would be gone for good.

'You can have her,' I said. 'But it has to be now.'

Dion wheezed and grinned, his tongue lying on his lower lip. Orlando grabbed my shirt, hauled me into an alley and shoved me against the wall. I looked up at him, my head swimming. The liquor had been strong.

'You're shocking keen to give her up,' Orlando said. 'What's in it for you?'

'Why, masters,' I said, knotting my hands. 'What higher hope could I cherish than to be of some small service to great ones such as yourselves?'

Dion, smirking, fitted a knuckleduster to his fist: a chunk of brass studded with rubies.

'Of course,' I added, 'among your virtues you are known as most *wealthy* masters, certainly far richer than my mistress. Perhaps some small token…'

Orlando nodded.

'That's what I thought.'

He brought his face close, staring into my good eye. Then he drove his forehead into the bridge of my nose. Cartilage snapped and the back of my head cracked on the bricks.

'Thanks, old clown,' Orlando said. 'But we know the way.'

He stepped back, and Dion slammed his knuckleduster into my sternum. I fell, unable to breathe and already growing distant from events as the Trelawney brothers' boots found my ribs, my hip, my neck. I lay and contemplated the night-glow of the city and the warm flow through my sinuses, wondering about the damage, wondering when I could rest. Soon, I thought. Orlando Trelawney tossed a silver coin onto my chest and walked away.

> • <

The room had no windows. There was a Judas hole in the door. Half-light filtered from a shaft in the ceiling, enough to show me the bucket in the corner, the fetters on my ankles, the dried blood on my rags.

For the first hours I lay on the dirt floor, nursing my bruises and trying to piece together how I had come to be here. I remembered the revellers passing me where I lay in the alley, most ignoring me, others laughing or applauding what they took to be my intoxication. Quick hands had helped themselves to Joanna's purse, and a little later a high-spirited group had relieved me of my mask and my wand. Later still, a lantern shone in my face and a man squatted beside me while another stood behind him, leaning on a halberd. I tried to get up, doing my best to seem like a citizen who had been taking a short rest and was now ready to go about his business, but one of the watchmen grasped my right hand and pulled off my cotton glove to expose the mark of the House of Montresor.

In time the light from the shaft grew bright enough to show the stains on the walls. A runnel of water coursed down the bricks, and I found that by putting my lips to it and sucking I could slake my thirst. Of my aches, the one that concerned me most was the deep pain in my eye. I could not seem to focus. I leaned my back against the wall, and after a time the light began to fade again. Hunger-cramps came and went. Perhaps no one would ever open the door, I thought. Perhaps I was to be forgotten. Longing for someone to come, dreading what it would mean if they did, I curled up on the floor as the last of the light died.

When I woke the room was murkily visible and the pain in my eye had eased. I drank from the wet bricks and settled myself in the corner of the room furthest from the door. The cramps in my gut were competing with the aching of my bruises. I wished I had a deck of cards. I moved my fingertips across my face, probing the swelling, and winced at the way the bridge of my nose now shifted back and forth.

I was occupied like this when two big young men in purple livery opened the door and led me up corridors and stairs, into the light of the great courtyard at the centre of the Montresor house.

A huge rectangular carpet had been unrolled in the courtyard, and on it an impromptu drawing room had been arranged, with tall plants in brass pots set among tables and cabinets of dark, glossy wood. Two straight-backed armchairs were occupied by a handsome couple in middle age. The man was bulky in his brocade coat, with a gold chain lying on his chest and his hands folded on his broad belly. His face was that of a well-fed old lion, with thick grey hair brushed back from the forehead. The woman was a poised, well-preserved lady, beautifully dressed in dark blue velvet with a brooch at her throat. Her eyelids were heavy and her brows arched in an expression of imperturbable calm. I stared for a long time before I truly understood that she was Isabella.

The Montresors were dealing with the petitions of lower sorts. One by one, tenants and other commoners were called forward from a small foot-shuffling crowd to wring their caps and beg their boons. Now that I had recognised her, she was as familiar to me as she had ever been in the old days, in spite of the years that had passed and the finery she now wore. The curious thing was that although I knew her so well, she was nothing at all like the image I had been carrying in my mind all this time. She was my Isabella, but she bore no resemblance whatsoever to Joanna Fortune.

At last Zachary Montresor pointed at me, and one of the guards shoved me between the shoulders. I tottered forward, almost tripping over my chain, and stood blinking against the sun while the guard explained that I had been taken by the city watch the night before last. It appeared I was a trespasser who had chosen to defy the law of Wen and the authority of the House of Montresor. Because I bore their mark, I had been delivered here for the master and mistress of the house to dispose of as they saw fit.

Zachary Montresor smoothed his whiskers. Fine lines gathered on his brow. Isabella studied me, holding her face motionless. I tried to stand up straight, to lift my chin and meet her eyes. I was barefoot, dressed in torn and filthy motley. I stank. I was a wreck of my old self, ravaged by thirty-five hard years. Nevertheless, I was determined to meet her eyes.

Montresor cleared his throat and looked over a paper.

' Ah, yes,' he said. 'This one's life is forfeit.'

I was light-headed with hunger and fear, but a kind of detachment had come over me. I had reached the second turning-point in my life. I had wandered a long way, but all my wanderings had brought me back to this spot, and perhaps, I thought, it could not have been otherwise. It was time to settle up.

I met Isabella's eyes. Her face revealed nothing and her hands were unmoving in her lap. There was one last thing I could do. I was not going to apologise, plead for mercy or beg her to think of the affection we once bore one another. By holding up my head and meeting my fate without complaint, I could show her what all this meant, because if the tragedy was mine it was hers as well.

'Does he have anything to say?' Montresor asked, but I ignored him. I had come back to Isabella, and what they did to me now would be the last act of our story. It would be a sad story, but ours.

Her face betrayed a touch of embarrassment, I thought, or irritation. She leaned over to her husband and murmured something in his ear. Montresor looked at me with more interest than before, and then gave a bark of laughter. He looked at Isabella, and after a moment she began to laugh too.

'So it is!' Montresor said. 'You're quite right.'

They smiled at me. Montresor reached out to his wife and they clasped hands.

'Well,' he said. 'For old times' sake, don't you think?'

Isabella nodded.

'Don't let me see you here again,' Montresor said, as one guard gripped my shoulder and the other unlocked my fetters. 'Sentiment only goes so far.'

My legs weakened and the guards caught me before I lost my footing. As they led me away, I called out to the Montresors, begging them to reconsider, begging for forgiveness. My toes dragged on the cobblestones and my voice cracked and broke as I asked them not to send me away.

Joanna set a loaf of bread in front of me and a pitcher of water beside it. I ate and drank until there was nothing left.

I was seated at the long table where the servants of the Fortune household had eaten their meals in happier times. The house was silent. Joanna wore old clothes, her sleeves rolled to the elbows and her hair caught up in a scarf. I could no longer understand why I had taken her for Isabella's double. The resemblance had only ever been slight. Joanna was simply a young noblewoman, no one I knew or could hope to know, her face bright with purpose. She was close to achieving a great ambition. She placed her fists on the table and leaned towards me, and I did my best not to quail.

'You can leave now,' she said, 'or you can see it through.'

Later I stood in an attic bedroom, fastening the buttons of my servant's livery. The outfit was ridiculous, with its stiff high collar, silk tailcoat, tight britches and buckled leather pumps, but as I stared in the mirror, fastening my hair back with a ribbon and combing through my beard with my fingertips, I thought it almost suited me.

I spent the rest of the afternoon following Joanna's instructions. I made the dining room as presentable as I could, lifting the chandelier off the table and sweeping up the smashed crockery and glass. I rehung the paintings and lit candles enough to fill the room with warm, flickering shadows. The shutters were to stay closed and locked, Joanna said. While I righted the dining chairs, she spread a tablecloth and laid out silver, china and crystal: two elaborate place settings, one at each end of the table.

In the servery beside the dining room, Joanna had arrayed platters, salvers and tureens. She had spent the best part of two days preparing all the dishes. She was the hostess, and as for me, I must make sure to serve the banquet faultlessly. Some of the silver-covered dishes were keeping warm over spirit burners. Others were to be served cold.

'Our guests will be here soon,' she said.

While she was dressing upstairs, I paced through the empty rooms. Night had fallen. The silver gleamed in the candlelight. I sat down in the servery and dealt hands of five-card draw until the doorbell clanged.

I was pushed aside by two hulking men in black and silver livery. A grand couple swept into the entrance hall: Cassius and Bianca Trelawney. The husband was a tall man whose lean frame supported a substantial pot belly. His wife's long, pallid throat rose through a series of creased chins to a pinched mouth.

Cassius Trelawney tossed his cloak to one of his bodyguards, while Bianca fingered her ruby choker and looked with distaste at the gloom, the dust, the fallen grandfather clock with its face hanging loose. Cassius's upper lip had the same brutal twist as his sons'.

Joanna appeared at the top of the stairs. She wore a black satin dress, the skirts wide and rustling, the bodice studded with beads of jet. A short black veil screened her eyes. She curtsied to her guests. The Trelawneys allowed me to bow them through to the dining room. Joanna had rehearsed me in the proper conduct for a footman, and my every movement was stiff with servility as I drew back their chairs, shook out their napkins and poured their wine.

A few moments later Joanna came in.

'Your men are taken care of,' she said. 'They're resting now.'

She stood by the table with her hands clasped, smiling serenely. I knew my role. I slipped out to the servery and carried in the first course, setting a bowl of thick brown soup in front of each guest. Fragrant steam rose and my stomach grumbled. Cassius dipped his spoon into the soup and sniffed at it, then set it down.

'Where's yours?' he said.

Joanna bowed her head and replied that of late she took no sustenance except the tears she shed for her brother, her mother and her father.

'Besides,' she said, 'I count myself unworthy to sit at table with the Trelawneys. I am your servant, great masters.'

She had invited them to dinner, she explained, to beg forgiveness for the transgressions of her family. The Fortunes had been proud and foolish, and she herself had been the proudest fool of all. They had been justly punished, and now her only desire was to make right the wrongs that had been done.

'Mothers and fathers must never lose their children,' she said. 'They must be together forever.'

Cassius and Bianca looked at one another dubiously. Bianca twisted her soup spoon in her fingers. Then Cassius snorted, and began to eat. After clearing the soup plates, I brought in the other courses in succession: a salad garnished with delicate slices of pink meat, then a spiced stew, then roasted joints with golden, glossy crackling. The dining room filled with rich smells.

Eventually both the Trelawneys sat back in their seats, wiping their mouths with their napkins.

'Not bad,' Cassius said, and belched. 'Rather good.'

Joanna curtsied again, a nervous hostess embarrassed by praise.

'I wish you could dine here always,' she said.

The Trelawneys exchanged another glance.

'You poor girl,' said Bianca. 'Do you still have hopes of marrying my son?'

Cassius laughed.

'You'll find the terms have changed,' he said. 'Dion may not be so keen as he was.'

Joanna bowed her head as if she might be blushing behind her veil.

'Perhaps not,' she said. 'Perhaps we might ask him.'

'Ask him?'

'Your sons will be joining us soon.'

I leaned over Cassius's left shoulder to fill his glass. The candles were burning low in the corners of the room.

'But there'll be time for that,' Joanna said. 'The meal isn't finished yet.'

She signalled to me, and I brought out the final course: a big oval platter with a domed silver cover. The aromas of the banquet had made me ravenous, and I was curious to see what she had prepared as the *pièce de résistance*. I set it in the middle of the table, as Joanna had told me, and lifted the cover with a flourish.

The cover rang like a bell and rolled in a half-circle on the floor. Someone had cried out. I thought it was me. I took a step backwards. Cassius and Bianca were on their feet, their chairs toppling. Joanna giggled decorously, covering her mouth with her fingertips.

On the platter lay the severed heads of Orlando and Dion Trelawney, surrounded by a garnish of green leaves and radishes. The heads were alive. Their tongues twitched and their lips mouthed words. The eyes rolled as if they were trying to make sense of their surroundings. The elder Trelawneys screamed, groaned and vomited. Bianca was clawing at her own throat. Cassius lost his footing and fell against the table, sending the heads tumbling to the floor.

Joanna opened a drawer in the sideboard and took out the ghostwork blade. When she had finished dismembering Cassius and Bianca she set their heads on the platter in the centre of the table, then retrieved the heads of the sons.

Four pairs of eyes strained to follow her. Four slack faces registered only bafflement.

'Douse the candles,' Joanna said.

While I obeyed, she snapped the ghostwork weapon under her heel and tossed the broken hilt onto the table.

She turned the key in the dining room door, then broke it off in the keyhole. We stood facing one another in the hall, in the gloom of one flickering lamp, and when she lifted her veil her face was beautiful, justified, innocent. It was nothing like the face I remembered.

> • <

A short time later Joanna Fortune locked the front gates of her family's house and dropped the key down a drain. The house was shuttered and dark behind its railings and willow leaves. She wore travelling clothes: a dark green jacket of tough cloth, men's trews and stout boots, a small pack on her back and a plain short sword at her hip. I watched her from a distance, unsure whether to flee while I had the chance. Then she looked at me, and I knew I had hesitated too long.

'Jack,' she said.

My thumb worried at the edge of a deck of cards in the pocket of my duster coat. Now that Joanna had finished her business with the Trelawneys, she told me, she was for the Ghost. In all the generations of salvage, even the boldest scavenger crews had not ventured past the fringes. No one knew what kinds of treasure might be waiting in the true depths. Joanna intended to travel into the heart of the Ghost and find out.

'You've been a help,' she said. 'Perhaps I'll take you with me.'

Her face shone with purpose and I knew I was no match for her will. What she decided, I would do. My legs grew weak and my head light, and I pressed a hand to my sternum, gasping with the familiar pain.

At last I found my voice.

'Please,' I whispered.

She stared a moment longer. Then, relenting, she bowed and walked away. I leaned against the wall, waiting for the ache in my chest to ease. My last image of her was of a young woman walking as if she were free to go anywhere. As if it were impossible for her ever to grow tired.

The following morning I stood in the crowd waiting to leave the city by the Tunnel Gate. I had nowhere particular to go, but no good could come of lingering in Wen, and there were settlements within a few days' walk where I could hope to find a game. The stakes would not be high, but the play might be decent enough.

The gate was busy, and I inched forward among the other travellers for the best part of an hour. My back ached under my knapsack, my feet throbbed from standing and I was jostled from all sides, but I did not mind too much. I was beside an elderly woman with threads of grey hair escaping from under a leather cap. I admired her stout walking staff. We fell into conversation, and soon discovered that we had been born in the same year. We reminisced about festivals past. When we were finally allowed through the gate, we found our journeys taking us in the same direction, and we kept one another company on the road for a while.

SILENT VALLEY

Eoin woke in the night, crying for his mother. She had been calling to him again. I held him close while he insisted that she was waiting and we must go. After he settled I lay listening to the silence of the small hours, to the scrabbling in the alley behind the house.

Just before dawn I lit the lamp, packed the rucksack with our last tins, and filled the canteen at the water-drum. Eoin said nothing when I told him we were leaving. His teeth chattered while I dressed him. Out in the morning dark he would not let go of my hand.

We walked from Stranmillis to the Ormeau Bridge without meeting a soul. The bonfires smouldered on the Embankment, silhouetting the charred bodies on the scaffold poles. Witchfinding was on the rise again and every night new towers of pallets, furniture and tyres burned for the punishment of those found guilty of trafficking with forbidden powers.

These days I avoided our neighbours. The last time we went to market, as I was bartering paracetamol for an old woman's jar of peanut butter, Eoin had announced without warning that his mother was waiting for him in the Silent Valley. I hushed him, but the woman stared and made a sign to ward off the evil eye.

> • <

Grey dawn on the Ormeau Road. We picked through the gridlock, the cars, vans and buses resting on their axles, their windscreens blind with lichen. To our left, beyond the Ravenhill, lay the plantation zone that had swallowed most of east Belfast. It pressed on my awareness like a headache but I did not look.

The zones had appeared six years ago, soon after Eoin's third birthday. They came all at once, seeming to unfold from a hidden dimension. Some engulfed whole districts while others occupied a few streets or even single buildings. It was impossible to say more about them because they were immune to human perception. Once or twice in those early days I strayed too close to an interface and ended up with a blank in my memory: a region of magnetised dread that repelled any attempt at scrutiny.

Within a week of the incursion more than half our neighbours had gone missing, taken away, and a language of euphemisms sprung up among the survivors. We spoke of the *other fellers* and the *kindly folk* if we had to speak of such things at all. We had our rituals of propitiation. No one was foolish enough to handle money now or use an electrical device, and every house had symbols carved in the doors and bits of iron nailed to the lintels. Gangs broke the legs of those suspected of carelessness. A year later we were the only family still living on Stranmillis Park. Sometimes I thought we must have an unsuspected talent for denial, for not seeing and not speaking. Perhaps, I thought, it was this that had kept us safe.

Eoin clung to my hand and walked in dogged silence. Half an hour brought us to the ruins of Forestside, where we found that militia had barricaded the main road with shopping trolleys. They waved us forward and it was too late not to obey. There were seven of them, none older than twenty, shorn-headed, armed with hatchets and crowbars. They looked askance at Eoin, wondering why a boy tall enough to recruit was hiding against his father like a child. They questioned us about our journey but all they really wanted was the rucksack. A toll for our passage, they said.

In any case, we could not go back. They ushered us through the roadblock and watched until we were out of sight. We continued south past rows of vehicles as mossy as burial mounds.

> • <

The carriageway brought us under banks of forest and between crumpled hills. The light drained since daybreak from the overcast sky. We passed farmhouses and old manses defeated long ago by the weather, roofs fallen in. More than once I was sure of being watched from the windows.

Eoin trudged beside me without complaint. His lips were blue, but when I asked if he was cold he said he did not know. He did not know if he was hungry either. Once he tripped and fell but he made no sound as I helped him up. I told him to clap his hands and stamp his feet, though when I did the same it was no help to my numb extremities.

We paused near a dead petrol station on the approach to Ballynahinch. This was the first real town we had encountered. I told Eoin that perhaps we would find something to eat in there and some way to get warm.

We passed the Annunciation Grammar School, a hulk of scorched steel and concrete that had once been a glassy modern building. Here, under the supervision of the nuns,

Saoirse had shed her last scraps of childhood Catholicism and aced her A levels before leaving for university in London. We met there as students, moved in together soon after graduating and were staunch Londoners for a decade. It was only when we decided to have a baby that Saoirse changed her mind. In spite of her contempt for those nuns, she discovered that she could not imagine bringing up a child anywhere except her own part of the world.

When I told English friends and colleagues that we were relocating, most were baffled. Moving to Belfast, they said: that's not something you hear very often. They asked cautiously if I wasn't concerned about the politics and the economy over there, or about whether I would be welcome. When I mentioned the plans to our next-door neighbour, a solicitor in his sixties, he shook his head and told me I was making a mistake. They're friendly on the surface, he said, but underneath there's something nasty. You'll see.

Saoirse was pregnant with Eoin by the time we moved. I felt we were starting a new life. We had found a nice little terraced house on Stranmillis Park and I was glad to be free of London – of the commute and the expense, and of the delusion, as I now saw it, of being at the centre of the world. If I sometimes felt like an outsider, the compensation was seeing Saoirse flourish. It was not only the pregnancy. She liked talking to people on the street here, joking and laughing more than she ever had in England, using turns of phrase I had never heard from her before. All of a sudden she was involved in campaigns about secular education and cross-community government. She took the new baby on marches for reproductive rights and equal marriage. I realised she had been waiting for years to play her part in these fights. If I found myself a little homesick, I realised, it was my turn; and besides, I was beginning to feel involved. While Saoirse fed a seven-month-old Eoin I scowled at the TV news, at an English politician standing in Westminster and calmly explaining that in relations with Europe the principle of national sovereignty was paramount. Does he actually not get the irony here, I asked. And does he not realise that thanks to him my son is now significantly more likely to get blown to bits by dissident paramilitaries? What?

She was smiling.

That time came back to me as we stole through Ballynahinch. We worked our way along the high street, watching for signs of life, keeping in the shelter of the gutted shops. Eoin's fingers were limp and solid, chilled through the marrow. I was kneeling in front of him, blowing on his fingertips in my cupped hands, when somebody chuckled behind me.

We were surrounded by a group of men in balaclava helmets. They carried an assortment of objects: billhooks, shovels, buckets, lengths of chain. In spite of the cold all of them were naked from neck to waist, and each had the same pattern of scars across his chest: a word in unknown characters, carved into each man's bluish flesh. Before I could tell Eoin to run they broke my nose, grabbed him and dragged us into the town.

> • <

On the day Saoirse went missing we had an argument – or rather, we had been bickering all day, unable to settle on what we really wanted to fight about. I was in a bad mood, feeling sorry for myself, brooding about what might be happening in England. Communication at a distance being over, I had no way to find out what had become of my parents in Hertfordshire or my siblings in London and Hull.

Saoirse was trying to persuade Eoin to read to her. We were concerned about how long it was taking him to get the hang of books. These things still mattered, we told one another – now more than ever – but we could not make him cooperate. He acted much younger than his age. Sometimes I imagined that when the plantations arrived, something inside him had changed too: something had got stuck, some line of development pushed off course. I could hear Saoirse's patience shortening and Eoin edging closer to a tantrum. He was rocking and whinging, trying to wriggle away from her and complaining that he was too tired.

I was tired myself, my head aching and my guts hollow. When Eoin finally tipped from sulky resistance into a meltdown, bawling at the top of his lungs and battering his heels on the floor, I gave Saoirse a look to say she should have known better. She glared back. The arguments did not have to be restated. She had to push him because I did not bother. It was my fault that she was to blame. She pressed her fists to her temples and went into the bedroom while I began to lecture Eoin about how it was time to grow up. He could not hear me, but I went on, as though I could prove Saoirse wrong by scolding him enough. He lay on his side, face to the wall, growling and shrieking to shut me out. In the end I threw up my hands, got my kit together, and went out scavenging.

Two hours later I turned back onto Stranmillis Park. I had been over to the Lisburn Road, searching for likely pickings among the grand houses hidden away in those quiet streets, finding nothing. Then I had noticed the light was fading and all at once I could not understand why I had stayed away so long. How could I have left them without making things right between us? Once we were together we would be ourselves again, I told myself, and hiked home as fast as I could.

Eoin and Saoirse were out in the street. Both were motionless, as if fixed in place. Eoin stood in front of the house and gazed at his mother. Her back was turned to him, her arms raised in what might have been a gesture of protection or warning, or a kind of salute, and her face was lifted towards – what?

I saw it, I was certain of that, but afterwards I could not tell what I had seen. I could only sift through broken images: a form like an oak tree, a crown of flowers that were not flowers, a gigantic orang-utan shaggy with moss, a suit of medieval plate armour that had been left to corrode on the ocean bed until its surface rotted to brittle green lacework and bright corals spilled out at the joints. These fragments did not piece together.

The visitor towered over Saoirse and she walked towards it. I must have called out, because she looked at me. Her eyes were bright as it lifted her off her feet, pale green brambles curling around her waist. After that, all I remembered was the crackling of wet twigs as the thing unlimbered itself, the single uncanny movement in which it rushed towards me and was gone, and Eoin's solemn eyes as I faced him along the empty street.

> • <

We walked hand in hand on rising ground. The mountains were close, the foothills nosing in, and the road offered us to all the scrutiny the sky might hold. I felt we had been walking for many hours, many more than a day could contain, but I did not remember sleeping or stopping to eat.

My sinuses tasted rusty and my cheekbones were still ringing with pain, but I could not recover the sequence of events. I had images of blunt hands thrusting us down a passageway of corrugated iron, and Eoin falling into a yard with his wrists bound. A ladderback chair stood on tarmac blanched with frost. In memory Eoin's terror was a substance, thickening the air and spreading from him in waves that ran off into the derelict streets of the town: there they did not vanish but swirled and mounted into a rustling, giggling noise that swelled all around us, making the men pause and look about. I remembered him telling me to keep my eyes closed until it was over, and then the screaming and the beating of wings.

And now I found us walking. Eoin was setting our pace, leading me without hesitation as if the map in him was growing clearer. We had come to the mountains from behind, I felt: these were not the soft blue shapes that had hovered above seaside towns on weekend outings in the old life, but a landscape of steep access roads, hidden reservoirs, barren slopes, old engineering. It was not a landscape made for us.

The light had almost gone when we topped a rise and saw the house. It was long and sprawling, perhaps a kind of gatehouse, set behind a stone wall and a big iron gate with paint coming away in shards of pillar-box red. Unlike the other houses we had seen on our journey, it was not a ruin.

The tiles were intact and the windows unbroken. Eoin tried to drag me past, up the track towards the darkening trees. We had to keep moving, he told me, we were almost there – but I made him stop. I strained my eyes into the house's gloom, almost sure I had seen a flicker behind the glass.

I was treading towards the front door when it opened and a woman stepped out. Her hair had grown long. Her breath made a plume in the dimming air, and in the swaying light of a candle her face was strange as only the most familiar faces can be.

> • <

She stirred up the fire, let us peel off our sodden clothes and gave us blankets. She gave us potato soup and nettle tea and we ate sitting cross-legged on the hearth. The parlour was lit only by firelight and the sky outside the window was a ribbon of pale gold fading behind the trees. She stood by the mantel but did not try to come near. She watched Eoin until he grew shy and burrowed his head under my arm. A minute later he was asleep. She studied his face.

She did not know what her name was. She did not know how she had come to be living in this house, or how long she had been here, or how she had survived. She could not remember any time before this; it was as if she had sprung into existence yesterday, or at the moment we had come within sight of the house. When I asked if she knew us her brow creased in the way it always did when she could not make up her mind.

Reunions were a puzzle, I thought, half-awake. To meet the person you know best in the world after long absence and in an unexpected place: how will you recognise one another, and how will you be sure? I almost had the answer, but as she settled by the hearth to watch over us I felt the difficulty was too great.

When she woke me the fire had died and starlight grinned through the glass. She was grasping for my hands like someone suffering night terrors.

Is it you, she was asking. Is it you?

Yes, I told her, it's me, it's us.

I don't know where I am, she said. I think I'm not here.

She was shivering wildly, and all I could think to do was hold open the heap of blankets so she could curl herself in beside Eoin. We lay on the hearth, holding one another, unable to find words of comfort, until we slept.

> • <

So we have come to the Silent Valley.

This morning I woke in daylight to Eoin shaking my shoulder, and sat up, bone-chilled and disoriented, brushing away the dead leaves that lay on me like a blanket, to find that we had been sleeping in the open. I looked around, confounded. The house of last night had dissolved and we had woken in the archaeology of a house, broken down and roofless, given over to the weather. Crumbled ridges marked where walls had once been, and a stub of chimney stood like an ivy-wrapped memorial stone. Leaves lay heaped in the corners, glistening with frost.

We have walked up the short track from the house through the trees and the abandoned car park. Once this was a place for day trips, for families and new couples and ramblers wanting an easy walk. The remains are here – the lavatory block, the playground, the duck pond, the café with its picnic tables – but, like all traces of the old life, they have forgotten themselves. I have to stare a long time before I begin to remember what they are for.

Eoin leads me on, up the track, past other structures whose purposes are even more obscure: sunken blockhouses and great stone cubes that have no entrances I can see. The mountains surround us now, their high backs mottled with heather. An artificial chasm has been dug in the earth, a channel walled with stone blocks where a river flows over pavement far below.

We climb a broad, smooth slope, as steep and regular as the flank of a pyramid, and when we reach the top the landscape reveals itself. The glacial valley opens, granite domes receding into haze, countless mountainsides stepping in behind to deepen the perspective. It folds around us. The reservoir is brimming, the vast black body of the water barely ruffled by the wind, reaching far between the mountains and out of sight. The spillway shaft is a funnel plunging into the dark. The water bursts into whiteness as it cascades down the ancient brickwork and I can hear the roar.

We are climbing the first mountainside, wading through heather and gorse. We look down on the reservoir and it is already small enough to cover with my hand. These mountains that were a prospect in the distance are now the ground under my feet. I cannot find the moment at which one becomes the other, but it keeps happening as we push on along the valley. My knees ache and I think Eoin must tire soon, but he is pulling ahead, gaining vigour as we go.

When I pause to get my breath he does not stop, and I hasten not to be left behind.

Often I think we are coming to a crest or a summit – a place where we can rest and see the whole landscape spread below – but when we get there another prospect opens and we have to keep climbing. Perspective shifts and the distance withdraws. Eoin walks on, and when I ask where he is heading he does not hear.

The question has no answer. I am not to ask where we have come from or where she is to be found. Eoin strides into the mountains, fast and strong, and my task is to follow him. Now that we are here we will always be here. We are always going further in. We walk, and we will walk, until all we are is walking.

ACKNOWLEDGEMENTS

Caoileann, Oisín, Odhrán and Sadhbh: all my love and thanks. For more help, encouragement, opportunity and support than I can measure, thank you Dan, Jenny, James, Andrew, Jane, Alec, Carey, Mima, Windsor, Toby, Pippa, Lily, Holly, Bernie. Thank you Jim: we miss you and I hope you would be pleased. Thank you Michelle Ryan, Ronan Crowley, Bryan Radley, Deborah Friedell, Darran McCann. Thank you Ian Sansom, David Torrans, Emma Warnock, Michael Nolan, Alessia Troisi, Reggie Chamberlain-King, Nicholas Royle, Greg McCartney, Michael Shannon. Thanks to Eleanor Birne and all at PEW Literary. Thanks to Dan Coxon and all at Unsung Stories. Special thanks to Nina Allan and Christopher Priest, without whom this book would not exist.

PUBLICATION HISTORY

Some of the stories in this collection were previously published in slightly different forms.

'Where You Are'
First broadcast on
BBC Radio 4 Short Works
(2019)

'In Phases'
First published in
Fictive Dream (2018)

'Pilgrim: Hinterlands'
First published in
Subtle Fiction (2018)

'Eurydice Box'
First published in
The Tangerine (2019)

'The Monstrosity in Love'
First published in
Black Static (2018)

'We Have Been To A
Marvellous Party'
First published in
The Honest Ulsterman (2021)

'Seafront Gothic'
First published in *Still Worlds
Turning*, No Alibis Press
(2019), Emma Warnock (ed.)

'Dangerous House'
First published in *Flash
Fiction* (2018)

'Bloodybones Jones'
First published in *Out of the
Darkness*, Unsung Stories
(2021), Dan Coxon (ed.)

'The Walker'
First published by the British
Science Fiction Association
online (2013)

'The Heights of Sleep'
First published in *MIROnline*
(2018); reprinted in *Best
British Short Stories 2019*,
Salt Publishing (2019),
Nicholas Royle (ed.)

'You Must Leave All Your
Belongings Behind'
First published in
London and Newcastle (2021)

'Silent Valley'
First published in *The Black
Dreams*, Blackstaff Press (2021),
Reggie Chamberlain-King (ed.)

ABOUT THE AUTHOR

Sam Thompson was born in London and now lives in Belfast. He is the author of two novels: *Communion Town*, which was longlisted for the 2012 Man Booker Prize, and *Jott*, which was shortlisted for the 2019 Encore Prize. A novel for children, *Wolfstongue*, was published by Little Island in 2021. His short fiction has appeared in *Best British Short Stories 2019* (Salt Publishing) and on BBC Radio 4. He teaches writing at Queen's University, Belfast.

OUT OF THE DARKNESS

EDITED BY DAN COXON

Out of the Darkness, in collaboration with mental health charity Together for Mental Wellbeing, challenges some of the most exciting voices in horror and dark fantasy to bring their worst fears out into the light. From the black dog of depression to acute anxiety and schizophrenia, these stories prove what fans of horror fiction have long known – that we must understand our demons to overcome them.

In the wake of the Covid-19 pandemic, what began as a mental health crisis has rapidly become an unprecedented tsunami. The Centre for Mental Health has estimated that 10 million people will need mental health support in the UK as a direct consequence of Covid-19, with a staggering 1.5 million of those being under eighteen.

Edited by Dan Coxon (*This Dreaming Isle*) and featuring exclusive stories by Alison Moore, Jenn Ashworth, Tim Major and Aliya Whiteley, this collection harnesses the power of fiction to explore and explain the darkest moments in our lives. Horror isn't just about the chills – it's also about the healing that comes after.

www.unsungstories.co.uk/out-of-the-darkness

Follow Dan @dancoxonauthor

UNEXPECTED PLACES TO FALL FROM, UNEXPECTED PLACES TO LAND
MALCOLM DEVLIN

"Malcolm Devlin is one of our finest voices"
Angela Slatter,
author of *Sourdough and Other Stories*

In the exact same moment, all possible versions of Prentis O'Rourke will cease to exist. By accident, by malice, by conflict, by illness – Prentis will not simply die. He will go extinct. These are the stories of the journeys we take and the journeys we wish we'd taken.

Malcolm Devlin's second short story collection ranges from science fiction to folk horror as Prentis O'Rourke's demise echoes across the dimensions. Scientists, artists, ex-nuns, taxi drivers, time travellers and aliens – the same people living varied lives in subtly different worlds. Something unprecedented will happen, and it will colour them all.

Crossing multiple realities, countless versions of ourselves, and shifting backwards and forwards through time, these are stories of forking paths and unexpected destinations – of flying and falling and getting up to try again.

www.unsungstories.co.uk/unexpected-places
Follow Malcolm @barquing